Blind Just

When Clint Brennan interrupts two men kidnapping his wife Belle, he is shot and left for dead. But he recovers his senses and finds that his wife is gone and he has been blinded. Most men would have given up, but not Clint. Astride his donkey, he sets out with his faithful dog Mutt on the trail of his wife's abductors.

Belle, meanwhile, believes her husband is dead, and when a rich saviour comes to her rescue, the people around her suggest it's time to start again. . . .

A tale of violence, betrayal and lies – it will all end at Wedlock, amidst flames and bullets.

By the same author

Death at Bethesda Falls
Last Chance Saloon
The $300 Man

Blind Justice at Wedlock

Ross Morton

A Black Horse Western

ROBERT HALE · LONDON

© Ross Morton 2011
First published in Great Britain 2011

ISBN 978-0-7090-9142-4

Robert Hale Limited
Clerkenwell House
Clerkenwell Green
London EC1R 0HT

www.halebooks.com

*To Jennifer, Hannah, Harry and Louise, with love
And to Chris Walker, a true friend and inspiration*

Typeset by
Derek Doyle & Associates, Shaw Heath
Printed and bound in Great Britain by
CPI Antony Rowe, Chippenham and Eastbourne

PROLOGUE

BRUTALLY DISRUPTED LIFE

When Clint Brennan came to, he felt Mutt's tongue licking his temple and cheek. Maybe the dog had brought him back to consciousness. He opened his eyes and realized that the world had changed. It was forbidding and dark. In more ways than one, light had gone out of his life. He raised his left arm and stroked the animal's matted hair where the bullet had entered Mutt's flank; it had bled some, but the fur was now just slightly tacky. He heard the dog's steady panting and smelled his breath, but he couldn't see him. The brutal truth was that he couldn't see anything. He was blind.

His memory was hazy at best, so he attempted to take stock. The sun was up and burning the left side of his face, its position and intensity telling him it was about noon. He guessed that he'd been out of it a good two hours or so. He was lying on his belly and something was digging into him. Ignoring the pounding in his head that wouldn't go away, he rolled over and then felt the pain in his left leg.

Scattered shards of memory started to pierce his thoughts, flickering like a lantern show, but they didn't present a coherent picture.

The sun – or perhaps fear – made him sweat. Fear for himself, thrust into this unwelcome darkness, an unknown territory. Fear for Belle, his wife. Where was she? Why wasn't she here to help him now, when he needed her? As much as he wanted to worry about Belle, some hidden knowledge or instinct shied his thoughts away from his wife.

He felt his forehead crease with the confusion of his mind, and he raised a hand to the dried blood around his eyes and the bridge of his nose. God Almighty, but his head pounded.

Heaving a great sigh, Clint pushed away the dark foreboding that threatened to envelop him and eased himself up on to his knees. That hurt some. His hand touched the wound: he'd been shot in the thigh. When or how, he wasn't quite sure. Crippled and blind, with Belle unaccountably absent from his life, an all-consuming despair soaked into his bones and made his shoulders slump.

Slowly, methodically, he scrabbled in the dirt and found what he'd been lying on – his Winchester rifle. He gripped its stock. Perhaps it would be for the best. He didn't believe he could exist in this condition and it wouldn't be fair to abandon his wounded dog. With a heavy heart he levered a .44 rimfire cartridge into the barrel. 'Well, Mutt, I guess this is the end of the road for both of us.' His voice croaked and his mouth was terribly dry. 'You first, old boy, then I'll join you.'

Mutt seemed to sense his fate and shuffled closer on his forelegs, rubbing his wet nose against his master's knees. Trusting to the end.

An almighty surge of humility and grief overwhelmed Clint Brennan. He closed tight his unseeing eyes and swore. He couldn't do this: it was against everything he and Belle believed. In the three years they'd been married, they'd buried two babies out back. The heart-break and the tears were testimony enough that they cherished life, and mourned its loss. Life was precious, to be savoured, despite the aches and pains. As his father used to say, 'If we never had any storms, we'd never appreciate the sunshine.'

Lowering the weapon, he stroked his dog. 'Let's have a look at that wound, eh?' Then he laughed bitterly at his choice of words.

Gently, he ran his hands over the faithful animal's body; Mutt yelped just the once – only the single wound, then. He experienced another flashing image from his recent past. It was all coming back now.

Painful though it was, the returning memory helped to impart some kind of sense to his present predicament. The irony was not lost on him, that in his mind's eye he could *see* what happened. Terrible though it was, it seemed that it was going to be the last thing he would see in this life. If he was destined to lose his sight, and it looked that way, then it would have been more bearable if his last view of the world had been a pleasant one.

Clint Brennan remembered.

He'd been working in the fields with Mutt by his side. It was mid-morning when he heard Belle and other raised voices shouting from the direction of the house. Heart in his mouth, he grabbed the rifle and hurried, breaking into a sweat. Mutt, a collie cross, ran by his side. He heard the distressed braying of their donkey Beatrice then, moments later, he emerged from the thin copse of trees and hesitated a second, unable to believe his eyes.

Two men were descending the porch steps. Both wore sombreros but didn't look Mexican.

Belle's pale green gingham dress was torn at the front and she was being dragged behind the man dressed flamboyantly in black trimmed with silver lace. 'Hey, Trent, she's quite the handful!' the man said.

'Don't worry, Howie! I'll tame her soon enough when we get her to camp tonight!' Trent laughed, slapping his tight-fitting buckskin pants and making a crude gesture.

'No, you cain't – she's gotta be unsullied,' said Howie. 'That's the deal!'

Clint's face grew hot. He raised the rifle and aimed at the man called Trent. 'Let my wife go or I shoot your pal!'

Growling and snarling Mutt was already running ahead, launching himself at Howie who appeared to be hurting his mistress.

Even with Belle struggling against him, the flamboyant Howie was fast and drew his Smith & Wesson revolver with his left hand and fired twice.

The first shot hit Mutt and with a whimper the brave animal fell to the ground and lay on his side, quivering with shock. The second shot hit Clint's left thigh at the instant that Clint let loose at the unencumbered Trent; his bullet sliced off Trent's left earlobe. Horses in the corral whinnied. Someone Clint hadn't seen, over by the barn, fired a revolver and this shot hit Clint from the side, damaging the bridge of his nose, his forehead and his eyes.

In the space of time between receiving the two wounds, Belle shrieked his name then Clint heard nothing as he plunged into unconsciousness.

So much for memory.

Now he caught the smell of burnt timber and for an

instant his heart skipped with fear. But it wasn't overpowering enough to be their house. Over the years, he'd scrabbled over the burned out ruins of several homesteads, and the stink lingered for a long time – all pervading and strong. Belle was alive, Clint told himself. Settle for that, for now.

Beatrice the donkey brayed – sounded as though she was over by the corral. She'd have to wait.

First things first. He withdrew his knife from its sheath and held Mutt down with one big hand, a questing finger identifying the bullet hole. Then he gently pressed the sharp tip into the wound. 'Steady, old boy, this is going to hurt, but that slug has to come out.'

Obediently, Mutt lay still, whimpering faintly, as if he was having a bad dream by the hearth.

Finally, Clint prised out the bullet and Mutt yelped.

'You're lucky, old feller,' he said, rolling it between his sticky fingertips. It was a .32 bullet, he reckoned by the feel of it; less stopping-power than a .44 or .45. 'You might live yet.'

Mutt licked his hand.

He sheathed the knife, slung the rifle strap over his shoulder, lifted his dog in his arms, and rose to his feet.

By simply putting weight on his left leg, he sent pain jolting through his whole body. Fresh sweat soaked his clothes. But he maintained his balance, which wasn't as easy as he'd have thought.

He recollected where he had fallen. About fifteen feet ahead of him was the well. Slowly, each step agony, he paced out the distance then came to a halt. No obstruction. Must have estimated wrongly. Mutt lay still in his arms, licking his hand. He was surprised and cheered that he could smell the freshness of the water, so it was closer than the burnt wood. Heartened, he shuffled a half step forward and stopped as his knees pressed against the brick wall of the well. Pain lanced from his wounded thigh, cutting short any feeling of achievement.

He lowered the dog on the stone lip. 'Steady, boy.' His hands located the wooden bucket and there was warm water inside. He drank from the ladle, running his tongue over slightly cracked lips. Despite standing in the sun for some hours, the warm water was most welcome. Then he let Mutt drink while he untied his big yellow bandana – it was quite a shock to realize that there would be no more colours in his life. Don't dwell on it. He soaked the material then wrapped it round Mutt's haunch and fastened the makeshift bandage with a knot. 'OK, Mutt, that's you taken care of – for now.' He gently lowered the dog to the ground.

As he straightened up, his heart pounded against his ribcage and it was as if a tight metal band of agony constricted his breathing. He ached with overwhelming rage.

Clint laughed ruefully. If he could see, probably he'd have one of those red hazes in front of his eyes – not that he'd suffered from such intense anger in many a year. Those mountain man days were long gone – or so he had thought. Belle had brought peace and tranquillity into his life. And now she'd been snatched away.

He felt his body tremble as his mind's eye again pictured the scene. He kept shunning the thought of Belle's torn dress and instead concentrated on the appearance of her abductors.

Howie, the flamboyant one, had a crooked nose and harboured a thick black moustache under it. He was broad shouldered and slim hipped and carried himself with confidence. The backs of his hands were covered in black hair and dark curls fountained out of the top of his black shirt. He had long unkempt coal black hair and a leathery complexion. His sombrero was black with white lace trimming and he wore tooled black leather boots and gun-belt. Was he left-handed or was he comfortable using a six-gun with either hand? No way of knowing.

Trent was shorter than Howie and had shoulder-length blond hair. He wore buckskin pants and shirt; at least the shoulder of the shirt was now blood-spattered. Almost boyish, with button nose and a clean-shaven burlap complexion. And now he was missing the left earlobe.

The wide brims of their hats concealed the colour of their eyes.

The third man – whose shot had probably blinded Clint – was a complete mystery. Even now he could still hear the sound of the shot that blinded him; very much like Howie's, he reckoned; not that it mattered a damn.

So he would know the first two if he saw – then he waylaid that thought and gritted his teeth, realizing that he was being stupid. He could give a fair description of Howie and Trent to Sheriff Latimer, but he couldn't identify them even if they were apprehended.

The dull and insistent ache in his left thigh reminded him that he needed to take care of that wound. Or he'd either get blood poisoning or bleed to death.

Was that such a bad thing?

He shrugged off that treacherous thought. By some means, he had to rescue Belle. He didn't quite know how he would achieve that in his parlous state, but he'd die trying rather than succumb to self-pity and maudlin moods.

'Come on, Mutt, let's get inside,' he said, moving his sound leg forward. The stabbing pain was bad but he

11

could bear it if he clenched his teeth, and he gained a little relief when his good leg took the weight. So, it was only really bad every other step. Think about the good steps, he told himself sternly, ignore the bad ones. Yeah, sure.

Mutt barked a few paces ahead. Encouraging.

The poor dog was wounded too. And he wasn't complaining.

Yeah, but he has four legs.

Stop griping and walk, damn you!

Clint walked. And at each small agonizing step more sweat erupted. At this rate, he opined, I'll be able to swim to the porch.

He stopped and listened. His breathing was ragged; he was parched, as the sun seemed to drain him of all moisture. But he distinctly heard Mutt's feet on the planks, his claws scuffing as he moved. Close, then. Shade was in sight. No, wrong – shade was within reach.

The boot toe of his injured leg stubbed the first step of the porch and he swore as the pain lanced into his vitals. That stab had been bad. He'd sensed the blood drain from his face and he'd swayed, as if he was going to faint. To steady himself he reached out with his right hand and found a firm wooden post that supported the porch roof.

With extreme effort, he forced his breathing back to some semblance of normality and raised one foot then the other on to the first step. This was going to take a long time – the simple act of walking up the steps of his home. He swore again. Might as well get the cussing out of the way now, he thought. He'd vowed never to use such language in their house and he wasn't much good at breaking a solemn promise.

Mutt made a keening sound, muted distress. 'Stay, boy,'

Clint commanded. He heard the dog lower himself on his haunches and let out a snuffle through its nose.

The doorway was more or less directly ahead of the steps. He strode towards it and touched the partly open door. He smelled damp earth to his right and glanced that way, nostrils dilating. For Belle's twenty-fifth birthday he'd bought a small round table and she'd put it by the door and placed on it a plant-pot festooned with gardenias. He smelled the flowers and pursed his lips as his foot trod on a broken sliver of pot and spilt soil.

Cautiously now, he entered his home. While he knew where all the pieces of furniture were supposed to be, he trod with care since it was likely that those men had disturbed more than a plant-pot of gardenias when they brutally disrupted his life.

CHAPTER ONE

A KILLING TO DO

Life changed for more people than just Clint Brennan that day. Some hours earlier, the townsfolk, as was their habit, got ready for yet another normal workday and gradually animated the streets of Bethesda Falls.

The bank owner and manager, Eustace Hayes bustled along Main Street on his way from his luxurious home at the top eastern end of town. He was on foot, as he had no wish for horseflesh to taint his best grey pinstripe suit, which he wore in readiness for an important meeting with the Chamber of Commerce worthies in the meeting rooms at the back of the Mayor's office. These rooms doubled up as the courthouse but today's business was purely commercial and, by the lights of some, not necessarily legal. He glanced briefly, almost guiltily, at the small bronze statue atop the building's gable: blind Lady Justice holding the scales in one hand and a sword in the other. Mayor Pringle had argued it was a waste of the town's money, especially since the woman wouldn't be able to see to punish the malefactors or accurately read the scales.

The Mayor lost the vote, however.

Overweight and out of shape, Hayes gasped for breath by the time he ascended the marble steps. Here he halted to compose himself and ease his heart back to its regular pace. He removed his hat, wiped his damp brow and ran a hand over his unruly and thinning blond hair. While he replaced his hat, he glanced at the imposing edifice opposite, Hayes Bank. His chest swelled with pride. Then he coughed, as he hadn't quite restored his breathing rhythm. Irritably, he checked his fob watch, its chain draped across his taut silk vest.

A tall broad shouldered sandy-haired man was approaching the bank.

Yes, the Chief Bank Clerk was on time, Hayes mused, which was only to be expected. Today, Jeremy Gamlin had the responsibility of opening up. Apart from the head teller, the remainder of the staff would not arrive at the premises for another thirty minutes.

Gamlin stopped walking and stood in front of the bank; he glanced up and down the street then studied the church clock visible above the rooftops on the corner of Front and Main. He consulted the timepiece from his waistcoat then climbed the granite steps to the bank door.

Hayes nodded. Ever since joining the bank some twelve months ago, Gamlin had proved to be both punctilious and diligent. The bank was in safe hands. Satisfied, Hayes turned on his heel, pocketed his fob watch and pushed open the double doors of the mayor's office.

Jeremy Gamlin was in the process of unlocking the bank door as the two men, Trent Dullard and Howie Rutherford, emerged from West First Street, which abutted the bank's brick wall. They too scanned the street before stepping up on to the boardwalk. There were a few passers-by but nobody paid them any attention. Their leader had advised them to leave their sombreros with the horses as that headgear was uncommon in these parts and would draw unwanted notice. So they'd purloined a couple of hats from pegs at Agnes Cassidy's Eatery earlier, after breakfast.

As they approached, Howie noticed a middle-aged woman step round the corner of East Second Street. She waved to Gamlin and called, 'Sorry I'm late, Mr Gamlin!'

His key in the lock, Gamlin turned and smiled at her. 'You're not late, Miss Wilson. I'm early.'

She drew alongside him and her lace-gloved hand patted the biscuit-coloured bun at the back of her lop-sided pillbox hat. 'You're such a gent, Mr Gamlin.'

'Nice of you to say so,' he replied then stopped as Howie and Trent came to a halt on his right side.

'Hiya, folks. Lovely day, ain't it?' said Trent, his tawny eyes sparkling.

'Nice day for it, I'm sure,' said Howie, eyeing Miss Wilson and taking off his hat.

Gamlin cocked his head to one side. 'Can I help you gentlemen?' His dark blue-grey eyes darted from one man to the next. 'Though the bank won't be open for another half-hour, I'm afraid.'

'Oh, I think it'll open for the likes of us,' Howie said. He rapidly drew a Smith & Wesson revolver and aimed it at Gamlin's belly. The six-gun was neatly concealed from view by Howie's hat.

Miss Wilson gasped and raised a hand to her mouth.

'Quiet, missy,' said Trent, leaning over her, 'else this here Mr Gamblin man gets plugged.'

'Oh.' Her face took on the same hue as the pearl

brooch at her collar.

Gamlin grasped her upper arm and held her firm, steadied her. 'Don't faint on me, Miss Wilson,' he whispered. He glared at Howie: 'You – you won't get away with this!'

'They always say that, but I think we will,' said Trent. 'Now open that door!'

His fingers trembling, Gamlin did as he was told.

Howie shoved Gamlin ahead of him and Trent pressed Miss Wilson to go in after them.

Once the four of them were inside, Howie slammed the door shut. The pane rattled behind the drawn 'Closed' shade.

'Now, who are you, missy?' Trent demanded.

'Miss Wilson is our head teller,' Gamlin explained. 'She usually comes in early to help Mr Hayes open up.'

'Well, it's her unlucky day, Mr Gamblin Man. . . .'

'Gamlin, the name's Gamlin.'

'Your name's what I say it is, feller.'

Gamlin swallowed and broke eye contact. 'Yes, of course.'

Trent took out his Army Colt .44 revolver and pressed its nose against Miss Wilson's heaving flat chest. 'Now, do as I tell you and nothing bad will happen to this lady, understand?'

'Enough of this,' snarled Howie. 'We've got a half-hour to clean out your bank, so make it snappy, Gamblin Man!'

Gamlin nodded. He looked at the revolver, spoke to it: 'What do you want me to do?'

Howie gestured with the barrel at the manager's office over on the right, behind the counter. 'Open the god-damned safe, you imbecile! This is a bank robbery!'

'Yes, right, I'll do that,' Gamlin murmured and fished

17

inside his jacket pocket for another set of keys. Shakily, he walked to the office of Mr Hayes and opened the door.

Standing in front of the large safe in the corner, Gamlin slipped the key in the lock and turned the brass handle.

As the heavy door swung open, the two bank robbers gasped at the neat piles of bills in their denomination label-wrapped bundles.

Gamlin glanced round at them and was unable to avoid Howie's sudden sharp pistol-lash to the side of his head. He slumped to the floor, his temple bloody.

'Oh, Mr Gamlin!' Miss Wilson's nutmeg-brown eyes looked pleadingly at Trent and he let her go. She rushed to the banker's side, knelt and cradled the man's head in her lap. She withdrew her gloves and used them to staunch the blood flow.

'Ain't that sweet?' Trent kept his gun trained on Miss Wilson. 'Hope you din't kill him, Howie.'

'Nope, I reckon he's got a thick skull.' Howie pulled out a gunnysack from the back pocket of his black britches. 'He'll be OK.' He threw the sack at Trent. 'Here, fill it up. I'll cover her.'

'My pleasure,' Trent said, grinning. He knelt in front of the safe and scooped the bundles of dollars into the sack. 'Hell, I can hardly stop my hands trembling, holding so much money!'

'Just get done damned quick, will you?' Howie snapped.

'Nearly done. . . .' Trent shoved the last bundle into the sack and stood up.

'Right,' said Howie, 'let's keep these two quiet.'

'Oh, my Lord,' whispered Miss Wilson. She closed her eyes and prayers tumbled from her lips.

Trent grabbed her arm. 'Put a cinch on your jaw, lady!' He withdrew his knife and its point pricked her cheek. She opened her eyes, the colour again deserting her face. She tried to crawl away. But his big hand clamped down hard on her throat while he proceeded to cut away portions of the hem of her dress. 'Lie still, woman!' he snapped. A moment later, he used a strip of the material to gag her.

Hauling Miss Wilson to her feet, Trent tied her hands behind her back and shoved her against the mahogany desk. 'Don't think of moving!' he drawled, emphasizing his threat by scattering the desk lamp, leather blotter and papers to the floor. She flinched and nodded, eyes wide and fearful.

Then Trent crossed over to Gamlin who was still lying on the floor. Trent tied a strip of dress round Gamlin's temple to stem the bleeding then used another piece to gag him. 'Up with you, Gamblin Man.' Roughly, he heaved Gamlin to his feet and pushed him round then tied his wrists together with a final strip of material.

'Are you done now?' Howie demanded, dragging the gunnysack along the floor towards the door. 'Time's pressing, damnit.'

'Yeah, that should keep 'em quiet while we get away.'

'Seems to me they'd be a whole lot quieter dead.'

The blood drained from the faces of both Gamlin and Miss Wilson.

'Thought crossed my mind, but we've got a bonus coming, remember, if we don't kill any bank staff.' Trent grinned, eyeing Gamlin then Miss Wilson. 'I was sorely tempted to have her on that there desk.'

'We ain't got time for that—'

'Yeah, sure, but that's easy for you to say, you're well set up. I ain't.'

'Then get yourself a woman – someone you can ride with.'

19

'I still fancy riding her—'

Howie swore. 'Will you quit that? Let's git!'

'OK, OK. So long, honey,' Trent called to Miss Wilson and waved.

The two bank robbers stood at the open door. Trent peered out. 'Nobody's paying us no mind,' he whispered. 'Let's go!'

They ducked out the door, shutting it after them, and walked hurriedly along the boardwalk and down the steps. Turning the corner of the bank building, they waved at a rider on a piebald at the end of the alley. A sorrel and a bay stood waiting, sombreros on the saddle-horns.

'We done it!' Howie called, discarding his hat and grabbing his sombrero from the bay.

'Quiet, man,' the leader ordered. 'Get mounted and let's ride. We've a killing to do.'

Leaning against the sill of the bank's side window, Gamlin watched the three robbers spur their mounts to the west end of the alley, which led to the fields, Yesler's Mill and Clearwater Creek. After a few minutes of rubbing the material at his mouth along the stone edge of the window, he finally peeled the fabric away. He gasped for breath then said, 'Are you all right, Miss Wilson?'

She nodded, her eyes still glistening with spent tears.

'Good. Then turn round and see if your nimble fingers can unfasten my wrists.' He shifted his position so his back was to her. A moment later, he felt her warm hands on his.

Gradually, patiently, she fumbled at the binding material and at last, after some minutes, he was free. Quickly, he untied her wrists.

'Oh, Jeremy, your head – are you—?'

'I'll be fine. We must tell the sheriff—'

'Deputy Sheriff, you mean,' she corrected him, her voice containing a tremor. 'How much longer is Sheriff Latimer going to be laid up, I wonder?'

'Yes, I forgot. Latimer's a wily old bird, even if he is still recovering from a gunshot wound.' He nodded. 'It looks like they're going to Rapid Creek, maybe Rapid City,' he observed. 'Jonas Johnson'll get a posse together.' He sighed heavily. 'And I'll need to inform Mr Hayes.'

'I'll stay here,' she said.

'You're sure – you'll be all right?'

Trembling, she nodded and glanced at the open safe door. 'What shall I tell any customers?'

'If they want to withdraw money, then they'll have to wait. Mr Hayes will wire for funds.'

She raised trembling fingers to her temple. 'This is terrible.'

'Yes it is.' He rested a hand briefly on her arm. 'You were very brave, Miss Wilson. Thank you for . . . you know, worrying about me.'

She nodded, her voice tremulous: 'I'm only glad they didn't shoot you – us, even.'

'Maybe that was their first mistake, eh?' He grinned and grabbed his black hat off the coat-stand and left.

Gamlin crossed Main Street and headed for the sheriff's office directly opposite.

Deputy Johnson wore his usual red checked shirt and jeans as he lounged in the sheriff's chair, his feet on the desk. 'What's up, Jeremy? Someone robbed the bank?' he asked, his voice thin and reedy.

Nodding vigorously, Gamlin removed his hat to reveal his bandaged bloody temple. 'That's exactly what happened, Jonas, not more'n ten minutes ago!'

Swearing, Johnson lowered his feet to the floor and

stood up, adjusting his gun-belt. 'Ten minutes, you say?'

'Yes, but they'll be long gone by now.'

Johnson's dun-coloured wide-set eyes stared in disbelief as Gamlin explained what had happened.

Again, Johnson swore, then grabbed his tan hat. The pair of them hurried out and crossed the street.

Miss Wilson emerged from the bank's doorway, wringing her hands.

'Are you all right, Miss Wilson?' the deputy called to her.

'Yes, they hurt Mr Gamlin, though.'

'Yep, I saw.' Johnson moved into the alley and studied the impressions in the dust. 'Yep, three horses all right,' he said, knuckling his hat back off his forehead. 'I guess we'd better give Mr Hayes the bad news.'

'Yeah,' said Gamlin, 'I was dreading this bit.'

They both climbed the steps from the alley and a short way along the boardwalk they crossed the street and entered the imposing doors of the courthouse. Their feet pounded noisily on the highly polished floorboards.

Johnson rapped his knuckles on the double doors labelled 'Meeting Room/Court'.

'Who is it?' It was Ralph Dunbar's voice.

'It's Deputy Johnson, Mr Mayor. I've got real bad news!'

One of the doors opened and tall cadaverous Dunbar ushered them both inside. The long tables formed a square u-shape with lanky angular Mayor Pringle in the centre, pontificating. 'Speculation is a good thing, my fellow citizens.' He tapped a chalkboard to his left, its black surface streaked with squares and rectangles and scrawled names. 'I do believe Mr Hayes has hit upon a highly profitable venture!' He paused and his cobalt eyes glared at Johnson. 'Well, Deputy Sheriff, what's so all-fired important?'

'The bank's been robbed, Mr Mayor.' Johnson glanced at Mr Hayes. 'They overpowered Mr Gamlin. . . .'

The banker's face took on an extreme red tinge. 'My God!' Hayes exclaimed and stood, jowls quivering, his voice distraught: 'I hold you personally responsible, Gamlin!'

Johnson chimed in, 'He was with Miss Wilson, Mr Hayes. He couldn't do nothing but obey their orders or they'd have shot Miss Wilson.'

There were gasps and growls of annoyance and anger from the other six men present.

Businesslike, the mayor asked, 'How many men do you require for a posse, Deputy?'

'Six to eight, sir,' Johnson suggested. 'Mr Gamlin reckons they lit out towards Rapid Creek.'

'Probably headed for Corrigan Pass,' suggested Dunbar.

'I'll round up the usual four,' said Slim Carney.

'Thanks, Slim.'

Dr Strang stepped forward. 'Let me take a look at that wound on your skull, Mr Gamlin.' He peeled back the dress fabric and Gamlin let out a plaintive cry as some blood had dried and stuck. 'It's all right, the bleeding has stopped. I don't reckon you'll need any stitches, anyway. Best medicine is to rest. You'll live, young man – though you'll probably have a headache for a day or so.'

'Gamlin's left *me* with a big headache!' grouched Hayes.

'You can wire for money from head office, can't you?' the mayor demanded. 'The business deal we were discussing, it has a deadline, you know. We can't wait.'

'Sure, it'll take a few days to get here, but we should still have ample time.'

'Well,' said Slim, 'if we catch the varmints who did this,

23

we won't have to wait any, we'll get back the bank's money!'

'Right, and that's what I intend to do,' said Deputy Johnson. 'We'll muster outside my office in twenty minutes.'

'I should go with you,' Gamlin said.

'No, do as the Doc says and rest,' Johnson said. 'Slim, tell the volunteers to be ready to travel for a couple of days.'

'Two days?' Slim queried.

'Yep. Even when we catch up with the robbers, we've got to persuade them to give up the money and that might mean a shootout or a siege.' His words sobered them up.

'Well, gentlemen, we'll adjourn,' said the mayor. 'Those who are joining the posse, I wish you the best of luck.'

'Thanks, Mr Mayor.' Johnson turned with Gamlin and they headed for the door.

'I blame that James gang!' Hayes said.

Johnson pivoted round. 'We don't know it was them.'

'That bank robbery last year in Liberty in broad daylight, it's bound to be copied by all sorts of bandits! My bank's proof of that!'

'I definitely need to lie down,' Gamlin said.

'Well, gentlemen, I'll be off,' said Johnson, shoving Gamlin ahead of him through the doorway.

'Please bring back my money – I mean, the bank's money.' Hayes sat down and put his head in his hands.

Once the three bank robbers had passed Yesler's flourmill and left the town behind, they headed into a copse of green ash trees that skirted Clearwater Creek. The road here forked three ways, north towards Grimm Mountain and Corrigan Pass, west to the Black Hills and south to a number of farmsteads some forty miles out, and beyond these the towns of Wedlock and Clearwater beckoned.

Now out of sight from any prying eyes from town, they stopped to divide the money from the sack into their saddle-bags. Then they turned their mounts south, as planned.

They approached the farmstead at a canter, not wishing to cause alarm. The leader held back, steering the piebald towards the barn. Trent and Howie rode on up to the hitching rail at the house.

At that moment an auburn-haired woman stepped out on to the porch, wiping her hands on a towel. 'Morning, gents,' she said. She wore a light green high-necked gingham dress and black lace-up boots. Her blue-grey eyes wary, she took a step back, near the threshold of the open door. 'What's your business?'

Howie climbed down from his bay while Trent sat inoffensively in his saddle, hands resting on the horn, smiling.

'Looking for your husband, Mrs Brennan,' said Howie, tipping a finger at the edge of his sombrero. His spurs jangled when he mounted the steps.

Swiftly, she took another pace back and reached inside the doorway, pulled out a shotgun.

But Howie was too fast. He rushed her and kicked at her hands before she could raise the weapon. Uttering a shout of pain, she dropped the shotgun and slumped against the wooden wall, nursing her hand, where a rowel from his spur had sliced into the back of it.

'That ain't no welcome to strangers, is it, Mrs Brennan?'

She raised her eyes defiantly to him. 'How'd you know my name? What do you want?'

Howie grinned; he liked her spirit. 'That's a lot of questions, ma'am.' He grabbed her arm, pulled her to him. He was facing her sideways on so her forcefully lifted knee only jarred against his thigh, not its intended target. 'Hey, you little spitfire, that hurt!'

'It was meant to!' she snapped between clenched teeth.

Forcing her back against the wall, he snatched at the lace neck of her dress and tore the front of it, revealing a fair portion of white cotton lace-trimmed chemise.

Trent dismounted and mounted the porch steps.

'That's enough, Howie, dear!' called their leader from the barn.

Pulling out his Smith & Wesson Army revolver, Howie levelled it at Belle Brennan. 'Don't you move!' he threatened then half turned. 'Just having a little fun, is all, Molly, darling.'

'Well, we ain't here for fun, or have you forgot already?' Her legs apart, Molly stood arms akimbo. She wore a split riding skirt of leather and knee-high boots. Her dark brown hair was frizzy and long, and blew in the slight breeze.

'No, you're right.' Howie scowled at Molly then faced Belle again. 'Get inside!' he ordered.

A hand clasping her torn dress to preserve her modesty, Belle kept her gaze on the six-gun and backed into the house.

'Stay out here, Trent,' Howie flung over his shoulder then followed her inside. He ransacked the kitchen, smashing a number of pots on the dresser. Then he let out an exultant shout as he found her earthenware jar of savings. He discarded coffee beans and valuable tea on the floor and ground them underfoot. Every desecration of the home filled him with glee as he watched Mrs Brennan slump against the inner wall, her body racked by sobs as she cradled her cut hand.

Abruptly, he forced her to her feet and along the short passage. He tipped the books from a small bookcase to the floor and kicked them out of their way.

He shoved her to the left, into her bedroom. There was hardly any floor-space, the place was cluttered with furniture: a tallboy, a rail with clothes hanging, a brass bedstead, the mattress covered with a colourful quilt, and a cabinet with an oil-lamp. Howie stood at the foot of the bed, holstered his gun and studied her.

Belle Brennan shuddered under his stare and he liked that. 'If it wasn't for Molly, I'd have you here now,' he snarled. He tipped the bed and mattress on to its side to reveal a shallow wooden chest. He knelt down, flung its lid open, but it was only filled with papers and photographs, nothing of worth to him.

Rising again, he pulled a long gilded mirror off the wall and flung it on the floor, where it shattered into dozens of pieces. She flinched, stifling a sob.

'Right, honey, you're joining us for a little ride – the ride of your life!' As he moved in on her she suddenly erupted, balling her fists, battering at him. Laughing, he deflected her blows and shoved her round then encircled her with his big arms. She kicked back at his legs but it didn't hurt much. He carried her awkwardly out of the bedroom, through the wrecked house and on to the porch. 'Hey, Trent,' he said, 'she's quite the handful!'

'Don't worry, Howie! I'll tame her soon enough when we get her to camp tonight!' Trent laughed, slapping his tight-fitting buckskin pants and making a crude gesture.

'No, you cain't – she's gotta be unsullied,' said Howie. 'That's the deal!'

CHAPTER TWO

ON THE SCENT

Belle struggled in Howie's arms, yet her heart lifted when she heard the sound of Clint's voice. Thank God, he's come in from the field. He emerged from the trees and stood at the edge of the hardpan, Winchester raised. He aimed at the one called Trent. 'Release my wife,' Clint shouted at Howie, 'or I shoot your pal!'

Everything was going to be all right, she realized. They'd have to let her go now. She smiled, seeing their snarling dog launch himself in the air at Howie.

Suddenly, it all went terribly wrong. Shucking her to one side, Howie pulled out a six-gun with his left hand and fired twice. She felt the gun's report and her body involuntarily jerked, as if the bullets pierced her.

Belle let out a cry as the first shot hit Mutt. With a whimper, the brave animal fell to the ground and lay quivering. Belle too was quivering as the second shot hit Clint's left thigh. 'No!' she cried, 'don't, please don't!'

In the same instant Trent staggered back, blood spurting from his left earlobe.

Horses in the corral whinnied and Beatrice brayed.

A matter of seconds later, the third member of the gang, Molly, raised her revolver and fired at Clint.

Seeing Clint's face suddenly covered in blood, Belle shrieked his name. Her husband's legs buckled under him and he fell face down in the dirt, unmoving. Her whole body felt racked with sobs; she was having difficulty breathing and Howie's tight grip around her waist did nothing to ease her distress. She struggled to pull away from him, to run to Clint, but Howie held her firmly and half carried, half dragged her across the hardpan to the barn.

Molly had brought out two saddled horses: Belle's chestnut, Yankee, and Clint's palomino, Taffy. 'Get her on the chestnut,' Molly ordered, holstering her Smith & Wesson six-gun.

As the shooting of her husband sank in, Belle felt weak and dazed. It was as if her life had gushed out of her at that terrible moment. Now, she stood trembling and disoriented while Howie tied her wrists and hauled her up into the saddle. She didn't care what happened to her now; her heart lay bloody and dead on the ground. She sat astride Yankee and without conscious thought shoved her boots in the stirrups.

Molly, now mounted, rode alongside and tied Belle's wrists to the saddle horn.

Starkly, harsh reality impinged on Belle's senses and she glared at Molly, recognizing her at last.

'What're you staring at?' Molly demanded, her light green eyes narrowed.

'You – you're Molly Nelson, from the Bella Union!'

'So what?' She raised her head, both cheeks flushed, a mole on the left. 'Think you're better than us soiled doves, is that it?'

'No. . . . But – but you shot Clint—'

'That was the general idea, honey.'

'Y-you meant to kill my husband?'

'He was just a man.' Molly shrugged her shoulders. 'They're all the same.' She leaned across, her hand squeezing Belle's cheeks. 'You're still pretty enough, I guess. You can get another one.'

Belle's stomach turned and she pulled her head away. But the repellent sensation of Molly's touch lingered.

Standing on the other side of Belle's horse, Howie scowled. 'I hope you've got kinder thoughts towards me, Molly, darling.'

' 'Course I do, love. Else I wouldn't have roped you in on this little caper, eh?' She winked. Then she glanced up in alarm.

Trent held a burning branch and was moving towards the house.

'Hey, Trent,' Molly called, 'stop that at once!'

Trent turned, grinning. 'I thought I'd torch the place. I like a good fire.'

'I know you do,' she replied. 'But we don't want to attract attention with smoke. The posse's going to Rapid Creek – there's no sense in drawing them back this way.'

Disgruntled, Trent flung the firebrand on the ground, where it sputtered and continued to burn.

Belle listened and wondered what Molly Nelson meant. *Posse?* It was terrible enough that Molly Nelson apparently intended shooting Clint all along, but now she wondered why Molly was running from the law. By all accounts Molly Nelson was joint owner of Bella Union, the bordello, so why would she throw that money-earner away?

She studied Howie, as he mounted his horse at the hitching rail, and her heart lurched. Barely a few minutes had elapsed since those two men had hauled up at that same hitching rail. Minutes in which her world had collapsed around her.

Was Howie the reason Molly was running from the posse? Perhaps it had something to do with what was in that carpetbag looped over Molly's pommel. And what purpose did killing Clint serve?

Both Howie and Trent rode up to them.

'Let's ride,' said Molly. 'We've a lot of ground to cover.'

'Where are you taking me?' Belle asked.

'Never you mind,' Molly said, taking Belle's reins and spurring her horse forward.

Howie trailed the palomino behind him.

Trent had started leading the donkey but the cussed animal was so obstreperous that he let it go. He drew his six-gun. 'I'll teach the critter—'

'Leave it be, it's done you no harm,' said Molly. 'Don't waste a bullet on it, we've had enough gunfire already and we don't want to draw any more attention.'

'All right,' he said grudgingly and holstered his gun. 'Damned critter!'

Howie laughed out loud till Molly used her quirt across his shoulders.

As Belle was led away on the chestnut, she glanced over her shoulder at the body of her husband lying next to their faithful dog. Her chest was tight and sobs rose to her throat. Her last view of Clint was blurred. She didn't have the will or the inclination to wipe away the tears.

Not long afterwards, a buckboard's two horses were pulled to a halt at the edge of the Brennan homestead. The driver's black hat cast a shadow over his face. The flat tray was crammed with a number of trunks and cases and tarpaulin-covered shapes.

Hunched on the front seat, he lit a slim cigar, all the while studying the still bodies of Clint Brennan and his dog.

He blew smoke into the air and climbed down. But he didn't approach the bodies; instead, he made for the house. For a moment, he paused beside a half-burnt branch, red embers still glowing in the blackened wood. Then he moved on, climbed the steps to the porch and walked inside.

Few minutes passed; he didn't tarry long and emerged empty-handed and flung the half-smoked cigar to the hardpan.

Clambering on to the buckboard again, he shook his head. 'What a terrible tragedy,' he whispered to himself.

Then, bunching his shoulders, he released the brake, shook the traces and urged the horses to move on at a gallop – west.

Now, some hours later, Clint edged his boots across the kitchen floor at a snail's pace, treading on discarded food and beverages, notably java beans, their smells surprisingly pungent to his nostrils. He bashed his left shin on a fallen chair, the pain accentuated by his wounded leg. Sucking in his breath, he leaned down to right the ladder-backed chair. Finally, a couple of steps further on, his questing hands knocked against the kitchen sink. Among the drying breakfast dishes, he found a cloth and soaked it in the washbasin. The water smelled of soapsuds. He rested against the edge of the unit and bathed the wound on his face. It hurt like hell. Gingerly, he fingered the shattered bridge bone of his nose. At least it hadn't affected his sense of smell; if anything, he seemed to be more sensitive to odours than before. He squeezed his eyes tight and opened them, but everything remained in complete darkness. He had hoped that maybe clotted blood had obscured his vision, but it must be more serious, much more serious. He wondered about his fleeting intention of ending his life. It would be utterly selfish, he knew. His main concern was not that he couldn't see. It was Belle's safety. Nothing else mattered to him.

He reached behind and tugged the chair he'd righted, then unslung his rifle, resting it on the floor next to the front chair leg. He lowered himself on the hardwood seat, left leg out straight. The washbasin was within reach. Slowly, he used the wet cloth to soak his wounded thigh. Judging by the pain level, it seemed that by some lucky chance the slug hadn't hit or broken the bone. The bullet was embedded in the thick and tough thigh muscle and had to come out.

Unsheathing his knife, he cut away a section of material around the wound. He dipped the blade in the soapy water then put the damp cloth between his teeth and bit down on it. Tensing himself, he fingered round the wound, each careful touch sending needles of pain jabbing into him. Within seconds, his face was saturated in sweat and water drooled from the cloth clamped in his mouth. He felt faint as he slid the point of the blade in. Judicious prising made his stomach clench and he hissed against the cloth in his mouth. It must be a .32, he told himself. Lucky as the dog, he thought. Eventually, he flipped the bullet out. He heard its light clatter on the floorboards. Then he slumped in the chair, panting heavily, fighting the swimming sensation in his head, which seemed much worse since he couldn't see.

Besides being torn by his clenched teeth, the wet cloth

was too short. He fumbled around the surface on the right of the sink and found a towel. He used the knife to slice it into narrow strips and lay one of these on the edge of the sink. He pictured in his mind where Belle kept her cooking ingredients. The man called Howie had clearly thrown many containers to the floor, but had he discarded everything? By touch, Clint moved along the dresser about twelve inches then raised a hand to the shelf above. His knuckles knocked against an earthen jar. The lid grated a little as he lifted it. He dipped a finger inside. Flour. He carried the container and retraced his steps to the sink. Now he sat down and lifted up the rifle, carefully ejecting and catching two shells. Patiently, ignoring the insistent ache in his head and the stabbing wound in his thigh, he used his knife to separate the bullet from its casing and poured the gunpowder on to the strip of towel. He repeated this with the second bullet then mixed in some flour and spit together. Carefully, he sat on the chair and tentatively by feel pressed the mixture and material over the wound, wrapped the strip round his thigh and tied it tight. He broke out in more sweat and hissed between his teeth as the astringent gunpowder worked on the bloody wound. Give it a little while, he told himself, his head feeling loose on his neck. Steady, control the pain. Let the bandage staunch the blood. He was impatient to get on, but his body had been badly damaged. Be sensible about this.

While he sat, he formulated in his mind what he needed to do and what he must take with him. The gift of Doc Strang's laudanum would have been most welcome right now, but the drug wouldn't only have relieved the pain, it would have sent him into drowsiness.

He jerked, his eyes opening, but still there was no light,

no vision. He still sat in the chair, supported against the table. Indoors, he had no way of measuring the passage of time. He must have dozed or lost consciousness, he couldn't be sure which, and it didn't matter anyway. His mind was made up. He could wait no longer and eased himself off the chair. If he used its back as a crutch he could hop and provide a little relief for the wounded leg. In this clumsy and noisy manner, he went through the kitchen and lounge and turned left into the short passage. Here he stumbled into some obstruction. The bookcase. As he righted it and gently piled the fallen books on a shelf, he remembered Belle's laughter. She wasn't prone to easy or frivolous joviality, but when she did laugh her whole face lit up.

'You know, I still think you're a secret book reader,' she'd joked when they'd been stacking the shelves.

'Really? Tell me, what theory is this, then?'

'Well, naming our donkey Beatrice – after the unrequited love of Dante's life!'

'Sorry to disappoint you, darling, but she's named after the town in Nebraska where I bought her!'

'Kill joy!'

Hugging her, he'd said, 'I only have two books – the Bible and Shakespeare's complete works – and they seem to cover pretty much all subjects I'm liable to be interested in.'

Clint let out a grunt as he realized the pleasure of reading had been snatched away from him too. He straightened up and clumped and shuffled sideways into the bedroom on his left and rested on the chair back while he caught his breath.

He was reluctant to abandon his support, but he remembered that the room was too small and cluttered for him to negotiate it using the chair. Letting go, he shuffle-hopped forward and immediately stumbled against something hard and metal on his left; his hands soon determined it was the bedstead. Upturned. That made things easier, he realized. With his good leg, he slid forward, following a floorboard groove and tapped his toe against the bedside cabinet. Stretching out his wounded leg, he knelt on his good one and shoved the cabinet to one side. The two loose floorboards lifted to the pressure of his knife.

Out of the under-floor cavity he hauled three bundles of material feathered with dust and cobwebs. They contained a Dragoon .44 six-gun, its cartridge-filled gun-belt, a sheathed Bowie knife plus a small leather bag of money. He kept the pouch and took half the coins and left the rest in the cloth, wrapped it up again and replaced it in the hole. Once he'd put back the boards, he raised himself up and rested the items on top of the cabinet, which he then moved over the hiding place.

Clint strapped on the gun-belt and tied the holster to his right thigh. The sheathed knife looped round his pants belt. There seemed little point in toting weapons, since he couldn't see anything, but strangely having them on his person imbued him with confidence, even if mightily misplaced.

To the right was their clothes rail. Hand outstretched, he hobbled in that direction. After two paces, his knuckles brushed against the puffed sleeves of Belle's liberty satin dress, which she'd worn at last year's Thanksgiving. It was a shimmering dark blue, he recalled. Eye-catching, she was, too, with braided auburn hair, cheeks flushed, blue-grey eyes alight.

Moisture rimmed his eyes and he knuckled it away as

his other hand found his buckskin jacket. He removed it from the hanger and shrugged his arms into it and pocketed the coin pouch.

On the floor beneath the hanging clothes, he found his moccasins. Their soft texture evoked memories of nights when he'd worn them to soundlessly hunt his prey, in the days before he'd met and fallen in love with Belle.

Now for the difficult part. He limped across the floor to the upended bedstead. On the other side was the mattress and bedclothes. He gripped the mattress and heaved it and the bedstead on to its four legs, barking his right shin as he stumbled backwards.

Kneeling with his right leg on the mattress, he moved his hands over the disarrayed bedding and located Belle's frilled long flannel nightdress. He held it briefly to his face, breathing in her familiar scent, and his resolve strengthened.

Getting off the mattress wasn't easy. He gritted his teeth and, partly rolling sideways, he somehow managed it. One hand clutching the nightdress, he stood and steadied his breathing, then with his free hand he touched the thigh-bandage. It didn't feel tacky, so maybe the wound had stopped bleeding, despite his exertions.

Blind memory wasn't too accurate, but eventually after a couple of misjudgements, he located the chair and clumped out of the room.

Next, he needed sustenance.

He lowered the nightdress to the kitchen table. A square tin was undisturbed on the dresser and he opened the lid, removed a dozen sourdough biscuits. He found half a dozen air-tights but had no way of knowing what they contained; maybe tomatoes, maybe condensed milk; he wrapped them in a cloth, which he knotted.

Remembering the salted ham that hung on the left of the sink, he cautiously moved over to it and carefully cut off a dozen slices and wrapped them in another cloth. He'd dearly love to take some coffee, but he could still smell the strong aroma underfoot. He barely managed to refrain from swearing.

Collecting the nightdress, his bundles of tins and ham, he moved round the table and shuffled towards the door. Together with a spare hat he normally wore Sundays to church, the water bottle was on the back of the kitchen door. He shoved the hat on and slung the bottle's strap over his shoulder, intending to fill the bottle from the well.

He limped on to the porch and he heard Mutt rise to his feet. Mutt licked Clint's left hand. 'Easy, boy. You've got a job to do. Real soon.' He moved slowly along the porch boards and gingerly stepped down. He caught the herbal smells of Belle's kitchen garden and an idea occurred to him.

He didn't have to go far and extracted a length of bamboo cane from the trellis of beans. It should help him avoid painful obstacles. His shins were bruised enough already.

The wound at his forehead itched but Clint refrained from scratching it. Maybe his hat rubbing against it didn't help, but he needed protection from the sun. He reckoned he'd been riding Beatrice for about two hours, or so the pain in his backside indicated. He couldn't remember the last time he'd ridden bareback. It was fortunate that the donkey and Mutt got on, otherwise he'd be stymied.

He'd hobbled to the barn but there was no sound from their horses. Gone, like Belle. When he called Beatrice, the donkey had obediently moved to his side. 'You're my means of transport, old girl. Treat me gently, eh?'

He'd given Mutt the scent of Belle from her nightdress, and the dog understood what was required of him. Now he sniffed the ground ahead. Attached to Mutt's collar was a length of rope that Clint had looped round Beatrice's neck. He couldn't have tracked them on foot, his leg was far too painful, though right now the ache in his butt was a close second.

To begin with he had an idea as to their direction – it seemed to be west. He'd half-knelt on the hardpan at the trail entrance to his homestead and lightly examined the ground with his fingers, taking his time. Fortunately, there'd been no breeze since their departure. The horse tracks were still fresh, four mounted and one without a rider – though it was puzzling that some of them had been obliterated by wagon wheel marks and the hoofs of two other horses. Why hadn't the wagon driver stopped to help him? Maybe the head-wound had appeared mortal.

This road gradually veered south and led towards the towns of Wedlock and Clearwater. As long as Belle's abductors stayed on the trail, he had a chance; he'd hunted round here for years and knew the country almost blindfold. Very amusing, he opined. If they hadn't stolen the horses, maybe he would have ridden into town to see the sheriff or his deputy. But that would have cost precious time in his present state, and he feared that time for Belle was running out.

CHAPTER THREE

SPECULATE TO ACCUMULATE

For the rest of the day, mindful of their horses, they rode south at a steady pace. Molly had insisted that they bring the spare palomino as, shared between them to spell one of their mounts, it might come in useful if they ever detected actual pursuit.

Howie trailed the palomino, while Molly led the reins of Belle Brennan's chestnut. Trent rode up front, scouting the way ahead.

They stuck to the regular route – since she reckoned it would be harder to track them on the established road. Though it seemed that their precautions were unnecessary; it looked like they'd gotten clean away. So far so good, Molly thought. One night in the woods, then tomorrow evening they'd be at the rendezvous, as planned.

Riding ahead of her, Trent cussed and complained as usual. A few times he turned in his saddle to ogle the Brennan woman. Molly let him; it was the closest he'd get, the fool.

40

She smiled. When the time came, Trent would get a bullet in the back and she and Howie could retire on the proceeds together. After the handover, but not before, she decided. Trent's gun still might come in handy if there were any problems.

Howie rode alongside her, smoking Bull Durham. She liked the smell of fresh tobacco, but it seemed the Brennan woman didn't.

'Smoke getting to you, honey?' Molly asked, turning in the saddle.

Belle Brennan wafted a hand in front of her face and shook her head. 'No, it isn't the smoke, Miss Nelson, it's the stink of your boyfriend's body.'

She's got spirit, all right.

'What the hell,' Howie shrieked, starting to rein in his horse. 'Why you. . . !'

Molly reached across and gently punched Howie's arm. 'Easy, darling. She just wants to rile you, and seems to be doing a good job at it, too.'

'Why'd she want to do that?' he asked, his muddy brown eyes liable to swamp her, like the Mississippi.

'It's in her nature, I guess. Treats us like school kids. Naughty children. She can't see the nice in anybody, least of all you, darling.'

Belle let out a bark of a laugh.

Molly's dark glare silenced her, though, and that pleased her immensely. 'Let's keep moving.' She turned and spurred her piebald. 'We want to make camp at Clearwater Creek.'

'Sure, Molly, whatever you say. You're the boss.'

'Indeed I am, Howie. And don't you forget it.'

Typical schoolmarm, that's what the Brennan woman was – stuck up and thinks she's better than our girls in the

Union. A mite begrudgingly, Molly thought the woman had worn well after two births; she'd still pull in clients if she were in the Union. That thought amused her some, then Molly scowled as she felt a hint of jealousy rising in her cheeks. Belle Brennan possessed that timeless look about her. Maybe it was her facial structure, the high cheekbones. She'd age slowly – unless she went to work in one of the godforsaken cathouses Molly'd been in, all very inferior to the Union.

Sure, the Bella Union money was all right, but it demanded long hours. And she thought her partner Grace wasn't to be trusted, either. No, she'd done the sensible thing and upped out of there while her own looks were still intact. And with her share of the week's takings, with the loot from the robbery to boot. Molly grinned, imagining all that perfume, those soft beds and good food to come. With more promised, as well. Best thing she ever did, to bed that crafty cold-blooded businessman. Howie mustn't ever know, of course; as far as he was concerned, the robbery and all was her idea.

Belle's thoughts kept returning to Clint. She tried to shake the hurtful image of him lying there with poor Mutt. If only she could think of the many happier times they'd shared; how they'd met, when she was a teacher. He came out of the mountains and wouldn't take no for an answer. Over a couple of years, he was just plain persistent, courting her. To begin with, she was set on furthering her career. 'I have my charges to consider, Mr Brennan,' she'd argued.

'It might sound a bit forward, Miss, but I'm not averse to having children of my own. Maybe to swell the numbers of your classroom.'

She'd flushed at his words. But in a way that clinched it. Not many men who'd courted her had given a fig for children. She sobbed at the memory. They'd thought themselves so fortunate. Little Jason was a picture, though he died after six months. Little Josie, she lasted ten months and succumbed to diphtheria. Their graves now abandoned. . . . Who'd refresh the flowers? She used the back of her hand to wipe the tears from her cheeks.

Reverend Dawson and his wife Rachel had been so good to them both and seemed to feel their loss keenly. By all accounts, Rachel had buried a child on their trek with the wagon train. Now she thought about Anna Comstock, who had taken over the schoolhouse. And Ruth Monroe who'd scandalized the town with her new beau, Deputy Johnson, a man some thirteen years younger than her. They were all her friends and now she feared she'd never see them again.

Who would bury poor Clint? God, the thought that coyotes or a wildcat might... She shuddered and her knuckles whitened over the saddle-horn while an uncommon hate burned in her chest.

Coughing loudly, Eustace Hayes paced up and down the meeting room floor. He should calm down, but he was dadblasted irate! And all all-important Mr Mayor Coop Pringle could do was sit at the head of the nearest long table and offer inane comments.

'You really need to settle down, Eustace,' said Coop, his voice smooth as syrup. 'You're overheating.'

'Overheating, am I? Well, for good reason!'

'Well, don't keep me in suspense.' He ran a hand through his blue-grey hair. 'Spill.'

'I've just been round to Gamlin's rooming house,'

Hayes said, wafting a sheet of paper.

'Is he recovered yet?'

'Recovered?' Hayes barked. 'He's up and left, the lily-livered swine!'

'Lily-livered. . . ?'

Hayes thrust the sheet at the mayor. 'Read it, Coop, then you'll know!'

Every damned word of Gamlin's succinct note was burned into his memory: *Dear Mr Hayes, I regret I must tender my resignation forthwith. I fear work in a bank is too dangerous. My apologies for not giving you adequate notice. Providing you don't make a fuss about my precipitate departure, I promise not to mention to anybody your land deal arrangement with the mayor. Respectfully, Jeremy Gamlin.*

'He knows about our plans?' the mayor squeaked, his sallow complexion taking on a paler hue.

'God knows how he found out, Coop, but if he were to go public, we'd be in deep trouble. Deep trouble.'

Coop cleared his throat. 'Well, it sounds like he won't say a word. He's gone – and, if you ask me, it's good riddance.'

'I suppose so.' Hayes finally lowered himself into a chair opposite the mayor. 'It's still a real worry.'

'I know, old friend, but you've got more immediate worries. The shopkeepers and farmers are going to need reassurance, at the very least. They're the backbone of our community.'

Hayes sighed. 'That's not the half of it. Businesses will go bust if that money isn't recovered. I know you don't understand business – but you've got to speculate to accumulate, and that's why we've got involved in our little scheme. Those same businessmen will be mighty pleased when the land deal goes through and their holdings quadrupled – well, maybe trebled.'

'Yes, I know, I've put money into the scheme as well, remember, even if it isn't quite legal.'

'No need to tell them the whole truth,' Hayes said.

'What they don't know won't hurt them, I guess.'

'That's it exactly.' Hayes retrieved Gamlin's letter from the mayor, folded it and placed it in his jacket pocket. From his waistcoat he lifted out his silver fob watch and flicked open the lid. Five hours had passed since the posse lit out. 'Maybe Johnson and his men have already caught up with the miscreants.'

'Five hours,' said the town's grocer, Ed Pike, as he glanced at his pocket watch. 'No sign of them yet, Jonas.' He sighed, running a hand over his shirt's left suspender. 'I reckon we're wasting our time.'

'Maybe. What do you reckon, Oren?' Johnson said, leaning over his saddle horn.

Oren Tatch, the blacksmith, held his horse's reins in one hand while he knelt to read the trail. He scratched his black beard. 'Reckon we're about two hours behind them.' He straightened up and stretched, his muscles bulging. 'We haven't gained on them. Four riders went north all right.'

'Four?' said Amos Jones. 'When'd three become four?'

'You're a right one to query numbers!' said Slim Carney with a laugh. 'You went and lost three hundred souls from our good town!'

'That was just a slip of the paintbrush,' Amos said in an aggrieved tone.

'Yeah,' said Johnson, 'I reckon the mayor was a mite harsh, giving you the sack for painting the wrong population numbers on our welcome sign.'*

* See *Death at Bethesda Falls*

'Seems to me,' grumbled Amos, rasping a hand over his whiskers, 'nobody wants to forget it.'

'Well, joking aside,' said Ralph Dunbar, 'I'm not sure I like the odds now – seven of us against four gunslingers.'

Malc Bodine said, 'We don't know they're gunmen – they didn't shoot anybody, did they?'

'They didn't need to – Jeremy and Miss Wilson were unarmed,' said Ralph.

'Hold on, guys,' said Johnson. 'We haven't been riding all this time to quit now. They stole our town's money – and pistol-whipped Jeremy and terrorized Miss Wilson.'

'That's right,' said Slim, 'but let's just go in cautious-like, eh?'

'Makes sense,' said Oren. 'If we rest our mounts for twenty minutes then ride 'em hard, we can probably make up lost time and ground.'

Johnson nodded and dismounted. 'All right. Give the cayuses a breather. Ed, you've got the watch, so tell us when fifteen minutes are up and we'll get on again.'

'Fifteen minutes?' said Amos. 'Oren said twenty.'

'Yeah, and we've spent five minutes jabbering,' said Johnson, loosening the cinch on his horse. 'Leave numbers to someone else, Amos!'

Amos scowled and turned away as his fellow posse members broke into laughter.

'We've had a good running streak so far, Kev,' said Bart Begley, his hat pushed away from his high forehead to show curly carrot hair. He pulled his roan next to Kevin Cafferty's sorrel. 'When do we start spending the money?'

'Oh, don't be moithering me so, Bart.' Riding stirrup-to-stirrup, Kevin raised a hand and flexed his long fingers and as if out of nowhere four playing cards appeared; all

46

aces. 'Be patient with me – it's a gift I have, you know.'

Pea-green eyes wide, Bart twisted his freckled face in earnest. 'But you still need me to hustle the gulls, Kev.'

'To be sure.' With his jet-black hair, flaring nostrils and bronzed complexion, Cafferty didn't appear to be a card-sharp, which caught many fledgling gamblers off-guard. His misty blue eyes sparkled with mischief as he patted the holster that housed his Buntline Navy revolver. 'And you've always got my back covered, friend, which is even more important.'

'Aye, we've had a few close calls, true enough.'

'Don't worry, I'll make a decision soon. Another town, maybe, then we'll have a few weeks off in a proper city instead of a flea-bitten backwater. Where we headed next, anyway?'

'Place called Bethesda Falls.'

Trusting to Mutt's keen sense of smell, Clint stuck to the southbound trail. Abruptly, he heard Mutt's distinctive snarl. Somebody was ahead of them – he heard now, it sounded like two riders approaching – and Mutt wasn't too keen on their company. He reined in Beatrice.

'What is it, boy?' Clint called to Mutt.

'Don't tell me, Mister, you've got a talking dog, is that it?'

The voice was over to his right, a little higher – a horse would be taller than a donkey. The man's horse tapped its fore-hoof on the ground, as if uncomfortable near an ass. The man's voice disclosed an Irish brogue.

Now Clint heard another set of hoofs, moving closer over on his left. He pursed his lips and hoped the pres-ence of these strangers didn't mess with the spoor Mutt was trailing.

'Howdy, strangers,' Clint said peaceably enough.

'Hey, Mister, are you all right?' the first speaker said. 'Should you be travelling alone? You look kind of blind.'

'That's right, I'm blind. A recent accident.'

'What a shame,' said the stranger.

'Come on Kev, let's go,' said the other one.

'In a minute, Bart,' Kev replied. 'First, I'm after a bit o' fun.'

'Aw, come on, let him be, will you?'

'Hey, Mister,' said Kev, the timbre of his voice thick with humour, 'do you want to be having a wee game of poker?' Clint heard Kev flick a pack of playing cards.

'That's generous of you,' Clint said, offering a smile. His right hand hovered over the butt of his six-gun, but he couldn't place with certainty where Bart, the other one, sat astride his horse. Then the horse blew air out its nostrils, close by, and Clint smelled the critter, but risking a shot would be foolish against two of them. He lowered his hand and decided he'd have to play along, even though the possibilities of this encounter didn't bode well and were at the very least going to delay him. 'But I think you'd have me at a disadvantage.'

'I hope you're not calling Kevin Cafferty a cheat, Mister.'

'No, of course not, Mr Cafferty. But I can't see my cards, so how will I know when I win?'

'Good point, to be sure,' Kevin said. 'I tell you what, let's dismount and spread out a blanket and have a game or two. My good friend Mr Bart Begley here will tell you your cards. He's an honest sort, is Bart. Can't be fairer than that, can we?'

Despite having a bad feeling about this, Clint swung his legs off Beatrice and stood on firm ground.

Mutt growled low in his throat.

'You'd better tell your dog to move off,' Kevin warned. 'He's making me uncomfortable.'

Clint heard a slow click of a revolver's hammer being eased back. He nodded. 'Sure, Kevin.' He knelt down and Mutt approached, licked his hand. He unfastened the rope on the dog's collar and whispered, 'Run off, boy. Run.' He gestured in the westerly direction, towards the creek.

The dog let out a short sharp bark and ran through what must be tall grass by the roadside, as Clint heard their stalks swished in the animal's wake.

'What's your name, Mister? Seeing as you know ours, like.'

'Brennan. Clint Brennan.'

'OK, Clint, let's just have a little fun to while away the hottest part of the day, eh? Nice shade over by yonder trees.'

'Whatever you say,' Clint said, and wondered why the man called Kevin didn't just simply rob him. Maybe he had scruples and couldn't blatantly rob a blind man, but he could dupe him at cards? Go figure.

Within a couple of minutes, Clint was sitting cross-legged on a blanket opposite Kevin; Bart sat or knelt to his left.

Cards shuffled and turned.

'You win,' Bart said. 'A dollar.'

'Throw in another dollar, friend,' suggested Kevin.

Coins chinked as the minutes stretched.

'Sorry,' Clint said, laying down four of his cards. 'Four of a kind – tens. I win, according to my memory of what young Bart here told me.'

'Nope – you're mistaken, Mister,' said Bart.

Even blind as he was, Clint detected the tension between the two men. Clearly, Kevin no longer wanted to play, he wanted to win by foul means.

'Are you sure?' Clint queried. 'I don't reckon Kevin can beat that.'

'Oh, but I can. . . . Four aces.'

'Well, that's mighty lucky of you,' Clint said and threw his fifth card down without further comment. He had no idea whether his own ace fell face up or down. He knew he'd been cheated but wasn't surprised. 'That's enough poker, thanks, Mr Cafferty. You seem to be having the luck of the Irish, so I must be on my way.'

'Oh, you shouldn't be leaving just yet, the game's just getting exciting, so it is!'

'No, I can't linger. Thanks for the entertainment. . . .'

Kevin exclaimed something in a hiss. 'You're just a bad loser, I reckon,' he added. His voice was closer now and instinctively Clint looked up but of course he saw nothing and nobody. But he felt the down-crashing force of hard metal on his temple and for a surprising but fleeting instant he swore colours flashed before his eyes. Dazed, he felt a second blow on his head and then there were no more feelings, no more smells and no more sounds.

CHAPTER FOUR

SURROUNDED BY DARKNESS

Fiery crimson slashed the sky behind a series of horizontal grey-brown clouds and the sight brought tears to Belle's eyes. Many a sunset she'd shared with Clint on their porch, content to be hugged. They gave each other strength to carry on, despite their grief. With the sunset came the promise of a new dawn, with the prospect of a future with healthy children and a thriving profitable homestead. All now dashed.

'Come on,' snapped Molly. She tugged at Belle's reins and led them off the trail.

A short way through tall grass and amid trees, they came to a narrow watercourse. Belle recognized it: Clearwater Creek.

'We'll camp here,' said Molly. A cluster of boxelder and elm provided shelter from the night winds and any chance road traveller's eyes. 'Leave the mounts saddled,' she added, 'in case we have to skedaddle quickly.'

'OK, makes sense, I guess,' said Howie and dismounted. 'Now, give me a hand with our merchandise.'

Between Howie and Molly, they helped Belle off Yankee, her chestnut. Trent led the horses to the edge of the clearing, hobbled them, and unfastened the bedrolls.

Molly shoved Belle hard against a tree trunk. 'You can bed down here.'

'Will you untie my hands?' Belle asked, holding her tethered wrists up in front of her. 'The rope's hurting.'

'No way, honey. A little rope-burn is nothing, I can tell you. You don't know how lucky you've been,' she said morosely.

Belle bit her lip and fought back tears. She didn't reply.

The creek babbled and chattering birds flitted, their dark shapes darting almost everywhere in the last moments of daytime, snatching their last few insects before night fell. She distinctly heard the sound of several chickadees. Somewhere nearby, a squirrel shinned noisily up a tree.

'I hate sleeping rough like this,' said Trent as he walked over and handed out the bedding.

Molly laughed and unrolled Belle's green bed blanket at the base of the tree. Then she flung out her own bedding beside Belle's. 'Don't worry, our days of hardship will soon be over,' she said in encouragement. 'Tomorrow night, we'll be in the shack.'

Howie said, 'Then we'll get our split, right?'

'That and more, you'll see,' she said and chuckled. 'We've got a deal and it's going to make us very rich.'

'I like the sound of that!' Trent said.

'Yeah, and in the meantime, you can dish up the grub,' said Molly.

'What, is it my turn already?'

'Yes, now stop moaning!' She turned on her heel. 'I'll get the food.'

While Howie retrieved twigs and logs for a fire, Trent broke out the pans and provisions from his horse-pack.

Molly moved over to the horses and unpacked a couple of tin cans of food.

Belle reckoned it was her only chance and took it. Smoothly, without any sudden movement, she slid round the bole of the tree and listened. Leaning her back against the trunk, she let out a sigh of relief. They were all too busy; nobody had noticed. Glancing down at the ground, she gripped her dress and lifted it slightly and stepped forward, avoiding any dried twigs. She tiptoed over the forest floor, and hurried behind a group of tree trunks. She glanced back. Nobody was following. No one shouted.

Now that she was out of sight of the camp, she ran a little, still careful where she placed her feet. No sense in tripping and turning an ankle. It was awkward running with her hands tied in front of her. Her motion was side-to-side, lumbering and ungainly, and she didn't seem to be covering much ground, either. Maybe she should find a sharp stone or something to sever the rope.

The creek had been on her left when she ran off, so if she kept it there – listening to its soothing trill over stones – and continued going, she'd end up heading north and eventually she'd come upon the Gilletts' farmstead. Not that she could hope to get anywhere tonight. Her immediate concern was finding concealment. If she hid long enough, perhaps they'd give up on her.

Her body tingled coldly as she recalled Molly's phrase: 'The merchandise.' What did she mean? Of course she'd heard tales of gunrunning renegades buying women. She thought they were called Comancheros, but they were a long way south, surely? Yet that was no reason why similar groups might not exist, just as lawless, just as willing to buy and sell women. Her mouth went dry at the thought.

'Listen,' whispered Oren Tatch. His big hands signed for the others to rein-in. Johnson marvelled at Oren. Sure, he was a big blacksmith, but he was also known for creating beautiful glass ornaments that those same big hands etched in fine detail. 'I reckon our robbers have made camp up ahead.'

Over in the trees on their right was the unmistakeable sound of horses whinnying and messware clanging.

'I could sure use a cup of black Java right now,' whispered Ed.

'If we do this right,' said Malc, 'coffee can go hang, we'll be drinking whiskey to celebrate.'

'That's enough chatter, men,' said Johnson, his voice hushed, his mouth suddenly dry as he dismounted. 'Zack, stay and hold the horses. We go in on foot.'

Zack nodded and stepped down from his saddle.

Soundlessly, Malc Bodine, Ralph Dunbar, Slim Carney, Amos Jones and Ed Pike dismounted and handed their reins to Zack.

The sun was setting to their left as they moved over the rough ground, off the trail towards the boxelder and elm trees. Fire-smoke curled up beyond the treetops into the darkening sky. Night wasn't far off.

A few more paces deeper into the forest, and suddenly Belle seemed surrounded by darkness. Night had fallen abruptly. She squinted, trying to see ahead, but it was difficult. Dark purple clouds obscured the moon. Ominous shadows enveloped her, leaves rustled. The sound of birds had stopped and now night creatures made strange unfamiliar noises. These were not the sounds she was accustomed to in town or even at their homestead. Sweat soaked the back of her dress as she stood stock-still. She was unable to move a foot forward, fearful she'd stumble into a tree trunk or fall down a steep dip in the forest floor. Oh, God, what could she do now? Pray for a break in the clouds? Pretend to be a tree, just like the game played in the schoolyard with the children? The rope around her wrists chafed. If only she could see just a little. But the darkness here in among the trees seemed absolute. And frightening.

Somewhere far off, a coyote howled.

At any moment she expected to hear voices and exclamations when they discovered she'd fled. But there was nothing like that at all. Maybe they'd already given up on her? She dared to hope.

Over to her left she detected the faint sound of the creek. If she made her way towards the water and kept it on her left, she'd be all right; all she had to do was head north. But the sound was quite indistinct. And was it really on her left? Slowly, with the utmost care, she moved to her right and listened – but now the sound seemed to be on her right.

Confused and flustered, Belle bit her lip and stifled a sob of frustration. She'd completely lost her bearings! She peered up and glimpsed dark segments of sky beyond the treetops, but the star constellations were no help. She supposed that Clint would have no difficulty at all stuck out here in the dark. Over the years he'd told her quite a few tales of his exploits. He was used to living in the wild, even hunting in the darkness. She trembled where she stood. Clint was dead. She had to face that. Had to live with that.

But she didn't rightly want to live. Another sob escaped her throat. She had no children to offer comfort in her bereavement. The homestead was nothing without Clint. Until he came into her life, she'd been drifting. Sure, doing good, enjoying her work, but emotionally she'd been empty. Clint filled that emptiness in her. Clint was her rock – now broken.

Five loud deep hoots erupted from a tree above her and she started out of her reverie. No need for alarm, she told herself, trying to calm her racing heart; that was a great horned owl. Abruptly, she clenched her teeth and straightened her back. No, Clint wouldn't give in like this. He'd fight. He'd find a way. She was being unfair to his memory, mewling about what she'd lost.

Right this minute, she was free of her abductors. A small but significant achievement. That counted for something. And if she could find her way back to a homestead and then the town, she'd testify against Clint's killers. If necessary, she'd devote her life to bringing them to justice.

Having made a decision, her spirits rose. She heaved in a big sigh, sank to her knees and slowly moved her hands over the ground. She shuddered as a couple of insects crawled over her fingers, but she persisted and a few seconds later, her right palm located a stout thick branch. About three feet long, she guessed. Rising up again, she gently swung the branch in front of her, tapping the ground as she tentatively moved forward. 'Steady, steady,' she cautioned herself in a whisper.

The branch clunked against a tree trunk and she carefully tapped at it to gauge how wide it was, then skirted round it. She was quite pleased with her progress and moved a little faster. She couldn't avoid stepping on twigs she couldn't see, and the noise she made sent shivers of apprehension up her spine, but she was consoled by the fact that maybe the night sounds of the forest cloaked the noise she made. So far, she couldn't hear any voices of pursuit.

At some point she might find some rocks to hide among, where she could even cut her bonds. She could only hope.

She had no way of knowing how long she walked at a snail's pace through the forest, but it seemed to be most of the night.

When the clouds scudded away, the gibbous moon's glow revealed she was standing in a clearing. The sky was brimful with stars. It was a glorious night, and she was free!

Then, her heart leapt as she spotted flickering light ahead, through the undergrowth. Someone camping, perhaps. A fellow traveller. She let out a sigh of relief and made to rush towards the light. Then stopped dead. Wait, she cautioned. Whoever was there might not be friendly. After all, she was a woman, alone, her wrists tethered. She might be stepping from one dangerous situation into another as equally troublesome.

When Clint Brennan came to, he felt Mutt's tongue licking his temple and cheek. Again. Or had it been a bad dream last time? He opened his eyes, but his world was still filled with darkness. With a heavy heart, he eased himself into a sitting position and shivered. It seemed that the sun had set since he was knocked unconscious. His first night of blindness – out here in the wild, in the darkness, not that it mattered much.

Again, he took stock. His head ached and so did his leg. Gingerly, he touched his thigh, but the wound hadn't re-opened. He was still wearing his shirt, his pants and boots.

That was something to be grateful for, he supposed. The bastards had drawn the line there, at least. Maybe that Bart fellow had made the difference, and not only let him live but prevented him from being stripped of everything. He'd never know. The money pouch in his pocket was gone, but they'd left his revolver and gun-belt – too old for their taste, probably. He pulled up his good leg and delved in his boot, on the inside leg, and pulled out the secret money pouch. He smiled, pleased he'd taken the precaution, and removed a couple of coins, put them in his pocket, then replaced the pouch in his boot.

Struggling to his feet, he patted Mutt. 'Bring Beatrice to me, old boy. To me, now.'

A moment later, he heard the donkey striding towards him and the dog nudged his wet nose against Clint's hand. Clint felt the rope between Mutt's jaws and relieved him of it. He brushed the hard bristly side of Beatrice reassuringly and palpated his bedroll and the saddle-bags. They'd left his moccasins, buckskin jacket, Belle's nightdress, the Winchester and two air-tights and a pan; but they'd taken the rest of his provisions. He swore then called Mutt over and tied the rope to the dog's collar again. He offered Belle's nightdress to renew the scent then took a few moments to get astride Beatrice. 'Come on, we have a trail to follow.'

Time passed and he had no idea how long he rode. His head swam and swirled with images and was filled with a throbbing ache. Eventually, he found his lids drooping and reluctantly tugged the animals to a halt. It made sense: his body was weak with loss of blood and the insidious continuous pain. He hated to admit the truth of it, but he needed to rest.

As he dismounted and staked out Beatrice, he wondered about Belle. He tried not to dwell on what those men might want with her. Despite his worries and concerns, sleep came swiftly, because he was exhausted.

In his dreams he could see. And he was walking an endless desert plain, the harsh egg-blue sky filled with sinister dark vultures that pecked at his rotten flesh; flesh that flaked off him as he dragged one foot after the other.

CHAPTER FIVE

THE SHACK

'Finished your walkabout, have you?' Molly asked. She stood a few paces behind Belle.

Belle swung round and gasped. 'I-I needed to relieve myself.'

'Sure, honey,' Molly said. Now she was wearing trousers. 'And it took you an hour to do it, and you walked round our camp so many times I lost count!'

Her shoulders slumped in abject defeat. 'I needed to walk,' Belle said. 'Riding all that time. . . .'

'No need to explain, honey. My ass aches after a while as well. That's why I've changed out of my skirt.'

Strong and tempting, the smell of cooked bacon wafted through the foliage. Belle's stomach rumbled and she licked her lips.

'Just in time for grub, I reckon.' Molly gestured. 'Come on.'

As the two women stepped into the fire-lit clearing, Molly said, 'You were lucky, honey, your dress is hardly damaged by your little adventure among the trees.' She

60

brushed a hand over the material. 'It'd be a shame to spoil it.'

Belle's hand clasped the torn front and drew it up to her throat.

On the other side of the fire, Trent stood up and grinned. 'We almost had bets on how long you'd take to find us again!'

Belle pulled a face at him and Howie let out a barking laugh.

She didn't care. She was starving.

Howie dished up beans and bacon on her tin plate and added two saleratus biscuits. Belle noticed Trent eyeing her.

Molly nudged Trent's arm. 'What's bothering you?'

'I'm itching to have my way with her, is all,' Trent said.

Molly sighed and lowered her plate. 'We agreed we wouldn't spoil the merchandise, didn't we?'

'So who made you boss, eh?'

'I did,' Howie chipped in. 'Molly's got the brains, so don't you forget it.'

'Yeah, and she has other things besides. That's what I'm talking about, damnit!'

Howie thumbed at the saddle-bags still slung across the backs of their horses. 'Molly has the contacts – else we wouldn't have all that loot, now would we?'

'Yeah, all right – for tonight,' Trent answered sullenly. 'But I'm getting awful itchy for a piece of skirt.'

'Then go scratch it yourself,' Molly said tartly.

Deputy Johnson removed his hat and scratched his head when he spotted the four bedrolls in the centre of the clearing. The small campsite was well lit by a stoked fire, dirty dishes and a coffee pot set to one side. Nobody was on guard. This was going to be too easy.

He straightened up and strode into the camp, his Remington revolver drawn. 'Come on, men – we've got them cold!'

The others entered the clearing and spread out, brandishing their weapons.

One of the sleepers woke. 'What the…?' He sat up and rubbed his eyes. Then he reached for his holstered gun at the side of his saddle.

'Don't be foolish, Mister,' said Jonas. 'My posse has you all covered.'

Malc kicked the boot soles of one sleeper, while Slim and Ed prodded their gun barrels at the other two. The three men slowly roused themselves and stared at the weapons levelled at them. None spoke but looked towards the man Jonas had woken.

'Posse?' the man said and slowly rose to his feet. He wore a green checked shirt, faded denim pants, scuffed rough-out boots and batwing chaps. 'What's a posse want with us?'

'I'm Bethesda's deputy sheriff,' said Johnson, walking up to him. 'We've been tracking you most of the day and I want to talk to you and your pals.'

The man was in his late thirties, Johnson guessed. Weather-beaten face, icy blue eyes, crooked nose and grey hair. His heart sank as he glanced across the campfire at the other three men. Not one of them appeared to fit the descriptions given by Gamlin and Miss Wilson.

'Talk all you want, Sheriff, but I reckon you've been following the wrong men.'

'Yeah, they all say that,' snapped Ralph.

'Mick, what do we do?' asked the brown-haired man covered by Malc.

'Keep cool, Larry,' Mick said. 'They'll soon realize their mistake.'

'Oren,' Johnson called, 'check their saddle-bags.'

'OK, Jonas.' Oren moved to the bedrolls. Keeping clear of the men lying down, he unbuckled the leather bags and examined the contents.

'Now, wait a minute, that's our stuff!' snapped a red-headed man.

'Leave it, Jeb – we've got nothing to hide.'

'Yeah, right,' said Ralph.

Johnson waited, sweat from his brow trailing into his eyes. 'Found anything yet?'

Oren stood over the last saddle-bag. 'Nope, there's no money here.'

'Money?' queried Mick.

'Yeah, we've just caught us some bank robbers,' said Ralph, waving his revolver threateningly.

'Steady, Ralph,' warned Johnson. He turned to the first man, Mick, obviously their leader. 'OK, Mister – what's your name?'

'Mick Hardacre, if you must know.'

'And your business?'

'Rustling,' said Mick, his mouth opening in a grin.

'See, I told you they were bad uns!' said Ralph.

'That was a joke,' said Mick.

'In poor taste, Hardacre. I could have you arrested—'

'It'll be a sorry state when a guy's arrested for joshing with the law,' Hardacre said.

'Yeah, I guess so. But sometimes it can backfire if you're faced with tired men with nervous trigger fingers.'

Hardacre shrugged. 'You'll find as many stolen steers as you will dollar bills in this camp.'

'They could've stopped on the way and hidden the

63

loot,' suggested Slim.

Oren shook his head. 'No, we'd have noticed. We've been on their trail all day.'

'Well, I'm glad to see somebody's got sense,' said Hardacre. 'As a matter of fact, we've just sold a small herd of beef in Wedlock.'

'Where's the money from the sale, eh?' snapped Ralph.

'We didn't hanker after getting bushwhacked by robbers,' he said pointedly. 'It's safe in the bank. It'll be wired to Rapid City for us to pick up there.' Hardacre shrugged. He patted the pocket of his jeans. 'We'd thought of stopping over at Bethesda to spend some of it. . . .'

'You can stay over now and bed down in the cells!' Slim said.

'How come you're bedded down so early?' Ed asked.

'It's been a long day. I didn't know there was a law against retiring early.'

Johnson pursed his lips then lowered his gun, holstered it. 'Sorry, Mr Hardacre, but it's been a long day for us as well. And it looks like we've been on a wild goose chase.'

'You mean these fellers didn't rob the bank?' Slim said.

'Their descriptions don't fit what Miss Wilson and Jeremy told me.' He shrugged. 'I had to be sure – they could've been desperadoes.'

'Since you've woken us up, d'you want to stay over for a coffee?' Mick Hardacre said. 'No hard feelings, deputy.' He extended a hand.

They shook.

'Yeah,' said Johnson, 'I reckon we might as well call it a night and get back to town tomorrow. I don't reckon Mr Hayes will be too happy when I report in.'

*

The next day, Trent was no happier. He scowled at Belle at every opportunity. Belle was grateful that Molly was a stronger character than Trent. Whenever they stopped to eat or rest their mounts, Molly made sure that Trent was at the other side of their little group. 'Don't give me an excuse, Trent,' Molly warned, fingering the butt of her six-gun.

'I'll bide my time,' Trent said and stalked off to roll a quirly.

'He's becoming a pain,' Howie whispered.

'Just don't turn your back on him,' Molly said.

The tension never seemed to let up all day. Belle feared what might happen if Trent got the better of Howie and Molly. He seemed to possess crafty features. Belle didn't like the way Molly kept fingering her dress, either. The woman had an acquisitive look in her eyes.

Clint rose with the warmth of the sun easing the stiffness of his bruised muscles. He pulled out Belle's nightdress and refreshed Mutt's sense of smell with it. 'Let's go, old boy,' he said and mounted Beatrice.

The scent led them south, in the direction of Wedlock, he reckoned. Why? What did they want with Belle?

To dispel dark fears, he thought to the times when they'd courted. She'd been a schoolmarm then. Popular and well liked, even loved.

Gradually, he battered down her objections to matrimony. Her acceptance was conditional, though, on the town obtaining a replacement. She was that dedicated. It took time, but when Anna Comstock took the post in 1863 – just three years ago – they finally became man and wife and he put the money down for their homestead and land – and the start of their dream life.

The solid ball of ache in his chest never left him entirely. Two babies dead. And frightened to try for any more. Doc Strang had said, 'Of course, there's always a risk during labour. But really there's no medical reason why you two shouldn't try for another baby.' Clint had fought Indians and fellow mountain men, chased a grizzly and once even outwitted a pack of wolves, but he baulked at putting his wife at risk yet again.

Now, it was a moot point. It would never happen. All he could hope to do was to rescue Belle, then go his own way and leave her to find another husband, a whole man who would provide a family and home for her.

Dusk spread its feelers over the land as Molly called a halt at the edge of a rocky clearing. About ten yards ahead was a slightly dilapidated shack with a split-shake roof, its log walls chinked with mud.

'We've made it!' Molly said.

'Home, sweet home,' Trent said without humour.

Inside, Howie built and lit a log fire, which offered the only illumination. There was only one window and door. In the far corner a cluster of mushrooms grew. Scattered around the hearth were opened tin cans, now empty, and three cups and a coffee pot.

Trent sat on the only bed. Light from the flames flickered on his features; his eyes glared at Belle, his face as if carved out of limestone.

Molly and Howie sat on two chairs at a stained and knife-scored wooden table.

'All right, honey, let's be having your dress,' Molly said.

Trent sat up straight and leaned forward, a curl to his lips.

'Why?' Belle demanded, her heart sinking. She cast a

66

wary glance at Trent and he bared uneven teeth.

'You've been otherwise preoccupied, I guess, else you'd have noticed the only luggage I'm carrying is that carpet-bag. I had to leave behind all those fine frilly silk dresses at the Union.'

'My heart bleeds for you,' Belle said.

Molly lifted her head, her chin pointed down at Belle, and her eyes narrowed. 'You're going to deserve everything you get, my girl.'

Howie chuckled.

As if struck, Belle flinched and moved her head to one side, eyes downcast and away from scrutiny.

'Your dress is a fine piece of material, Mrs Brennan, even if you almost spoiled it in the forest. It'll patch up as good as new. Now, give it to me.'

'What do you want her dress for?' Howie said. 'Soon, you can buy all you need.'

Molly let out a laugh. 'She won't be needing it, Howie dear.'

'Yeah,' mused Howie. 'Come on, Mrs Brennan, do as Molly says!'

'Yeah,' echoed Trent, licking his lips.

Feeling the blood rush to her face, Belle silently obeyed and unhooked her dress fastenings and stepped out of the garment. She flung the dress at Molly.

'Thank you, my dear,' Molly said, catching it. She spread the garment on the tabletop and proceeded to fold it carefully into a tight bundle. Then she signed to Howie. 'Now tie her up.'

'Aw, can't I do that?' Trent asked.

Belle stood awkwardly in her white cotton undergarments. Her eyes pleaded with Molly.

'No, we keep her unsullied, as I said. You do it, Howie.'

She got up and stopped at the door. 'Don't try anything while I'm gone,' she warned, the dress bundle clutched in her arms.

'We'll be good, honest, Molly dear,' Howie said.

'I'm serious,' she said and opened the door and slipped out.

Howie tightly tied Belle's hands behind her back, while Trent paced up and down, eyeing her. The rope chafed her already raw wrists.

Soon, Molly returned. 'The horses seem a mite jittery,' she said. 'Trent, go and check them out.'

'Why's it always me?'

'Because she's the boss,' Howie said and laughed.

Reluctantly, Trent pulled his eyes from Belle and slunk out the doorway.

He was gone less than five minutes. He rushed inside, slammed the door and leaned his back against it. 'Someone's out there, I heard them!'

Suddenly, three rifle shots sounded outside. The bullets hit the shack's walls.

'It's the posse!' Howie exclaimed.

'Get to the window!' Molly barked. 'Quickly, man!'

Hope leapt into her breast and Belle leaned against the back wall of the shack. She glanced around, but she already knew there was no other door. She recalled the hopes she'd felt when she ran away in the forest – futile hopes. Maybe this time she could dare to hope.

Abruptly, Molly stepped towards the fireplace and doused the flames with the remains of the coffee; the logs hissed and plunged the shack into sudden darkness.

Belle felt a sharp hard blow on her head and sank into unconsciousness.

CHAPTER SIX

RESCUED

Clint woke to the sound of shots, reached for his six-gun and rolled out from under his blanket. His heart pounded and he strained his ears, but the sounds were not near. No threat, he reasoned, and holstered the weapon. Definitely rifles. About two miles away and, he realized with a sinking feeling in his gut, in the general direction Mutt was leading him.

He stood a while longer, listening. Crickets chirruped, but there was no more firing. Was that a good sign? He doubted it. Running a hand down over his face, he took in a deep calming breath. He wasn't going to settle down again, he knew. He'd just end up pacing till the sun came up. It wasn't as though he needed daylight to see by, so he might as well move out.

He fished in his jacket pocket and pulled out a chunk of hardtack, cut off a sliver and chewed on it. After a short while, the juices slid down his throat and his stomach rumbled, expectant.

'Come on, Mutt,' he called, 'we're breaking camp early!'

Retrieving his blanket, getting packed and mounting Beatrice seemed to take an age and proved an almighty headache, but eventually he managed it.

Belle awoke with a pounding headache. She immediately realized that her wrists were no longer tied and raised a hand to the back of her head. She felt a small yet prominent bump, and it was sore. She was surprised to find that her right hand was bandaged.

Pale moonlight slanted through the shack's open doorway. She sat up and pushed aside a smelly horse blanket. Then she noticed she was wearing her undergarments and she remembered – Molly and the others – being attacked. . . .

Belle gave a start and grabbed the blanket back to cover herself.

To one side of the door, half in shadow, a man hunkered down, holding a hat. 'Welcome back to the living, Mrs Brennan,' he said.

She thought she recognized the voice. 'Do I know you?' she croaked.

'Name's Gamlin, ma'am. Jeremy Gamlin.'

'Yes, of course – you work at the bank.'

'Used to, ma'am. Quit after it was robbed.'

'The bank was robbed?' She had an idea who the culprits were, now.

'Yes. Seems to me, it's too dangerous an occupation.'

'But what are you doing here – and where are the people who abducted me, Molly Nelson, Trent and Howie?'

He stood up and strode towards her. 'Is that their names?' She nodded. 'And one of them a lady, eh?'

'She was no lady.'

'Quite. Well, I chased them away.' He held out a plaid mackinaw. 'This'll keep the night chill off of you till we get you to town.'

'Thank you, Mr Gamlin.' Back to town. The prospect should fill her with pleasure, but it didn't. She'd have to arrange for Clint's body to be collected, and get his funeral organized, and sort out the home finances. Sighing heavily, she pushed the blanket aside, stood and turned her back to let Mr Gamlin slip the coat on her. She thrust her arms in the sleeves. It was slightly cold against her bare flesh, but soon warmed. Turning, she buttoned it up. 'You haven't told me how you became my rescuer. I guess it was you firing at Nelson and her gang?'

'That's right. It's a long story – I'll fill you in on the way.'

'Thank you again, Mr Gamlin.'

They stepped out of the shack and a short way beyond was a buckboard, its flatbed fully laden. Gamlin helped her up on to the seat, then he walked round the back, checked the securing ropes and climbed up on the other side. The seat was so narrow that their bodies touched. She was mindful that she only wore undergarments beneath the coat, but he didn't seem to pay her any undue attention. Quite the gentleman, in fact.

He geed the two horses and they rode back on to the trail.

'Earlier today, I'd come out to your ranch, ma'am, on business. And I found your husband and your dog dead.'

She nodded and let out a sob, picturing again the scene she'd left behind. She glanced down at her hands in her lap; they were trembling.

He pulled out a metal drinks flask. 'Here, take a sip, it'll calm you.'

'What is it?'

71

'Brandy.'

'No, thanks, I'll be all right.'

'I'm really sorry, ma'am.' He screwed on the lid and pocketed the flask. 'I'm no expert, but it looked to me like your footprints led to a horse. Other footprints crowded yours. So I reckoned you was abducted. Don't know why, though – do you?'

She shook her head. 'No, but they kept calling me "merchandise", as if they were going to sell me.' She shuddered at the thought.

'I'm sorry about your husband, ma'am.'

'Thank you.' She didn't want to think about it. 'You said you came out to our place on business, Mr Gamlin?'

'Yes. It seems academic now, though.'

'Please, Mr Gamlin, humour me. What business brought you out from the bank?'

'I feel a mite awkward telling you now, ma'am. I don't like speaking ill of the dead.'

Her heart fluttered and her stomach lurched. What did he mean by that? She had to know and steeled herself. 'Go on, tell me, Mr Gamlin. Please.'

'OK, Mrs Brennan. Mr Hayes had a foreclosure notice all drawn up for your homestead and land. I came out to warn you both.'

'Fore – foreclose?'

'Mr Brennan built up quite a gaming debt, ma'am.' Gamlin shrugged. 'Sadly, I've seen it plenty of times before. He was gambling with money he didn't have.'

Her heart overturned and she felt faint. She gripped the side handrail. 'Gambling? Clint?' She shook her head. 'No, he wouldn't do that!'

Gamlin shrugged. 'That's the word I got.'

'Then the word's mistaken,' she snapped forcefully. 'I

think I will have that drink now, Mr Gamlin, if you don't mind?'

'Certainly, ma'am.' He handed her the flask.

She opened it and took a gulp. The liquid was fiery, strong and burned her throat a little. Seconds later, it seemed to hit her empty stomach and she felt a warm glow suffusing her body. 'Thank you.' As she returned the flask, she glanced at the night sky, the moon, the stars; Clint had told her what that constellation meant, but now she couldn't remember. Over on their left, illuminated by the moonlight, a trail marker: *Wedlock, 12 miles.* She shifted anxiously in her seat and half turned to face him. 'Mr Gamlin, you're not going back to Bethesda Falls.' It was a statement, not a question.

'You don't want to go back there, ma'am—'

'But I do! I need to bury my husband – and sort out this misunderstanding about his debt!' Despite herself, she felt tears pricking her eyes.

'That's not a good idea, ma'am. Not tonight, anyway.'

'Why?'

'I scared those varmints off, but I don't know if they'll stay scared when they realize it was only me and not a posse. They may be waiting back on the trail.'

Belle nodded. 'Very well, but when we get to Wedlock, I'll make plans to return to Bethesda Falls in daylight.' He didn't answer and then it struck her. She had no money with her and, in fact, no clothing. She glanced sideways at Mr Gamlin. He was intent on the horses as they negotiated a narrow defile, the wheel hubs bare inches from the rock on both sides.

She shook her head. Clint would never jeopardize their homestead. Though, she did recollect him saying he used to gamble with other mountain men. But that was years ago, when he was a much younger man. 'I've had an eventful and wild life, Belle, but all that changed when I set eyes on you.' She remembered the look of sincerity in his eyes. And he'd been true to his word. Or had he. . . ?

Finally, as the horses broke through on to a wide hardened trail, Gamlin broke into her thoughts, 'I'm going to start a new life in Wedlock, ma'am. To be honest, I've been planning it for a while. When we get there, and once I've concluded some business transactions to finalize things, I'll be happy to help you in any way I can.'

'Thank you, Mr Gamlin.'

'Jeremy.'

'That's very kind of you, Jeremy.'

Trent, Howie and Molly halted their snorting and heaving horses about five miles north of the shack. Clearwater Creek rippled on their left. 'We'll make camp here,' Molly said.

Trent snapped, 'I thought we were done with camping out at night?'

'Circumstances dictate,' Molly said, 'so we have to adapt.'

Leaning across from his bay, Howie clapped Trent round the shoulders. 'And soon we'll have to adapt to being rich – very rich!'

'Yeah, OK. I reckon we've earned a rest, after all that shooting!' Trent said, stepping down from his mount.

Howie dismounted and laughed.

'And we got away with the two horses as well,' Trent said, thumbing at the palomino and the chestnut.

'Everything worked out so well,' Howie added, helping Molly down from her saddle.

'That's why I'm the boss,' she said, planting a kiss on his cheek.

Scowling at them, Trent led his sorrel to a stand of trees and looped the reins round a thin sapling. He started to release the girth.

'I told you last night, leave them saddled,' Molly called over. 'If we get any more surprises, we want to be riding out of here pronto.'

'Yeah, all right. Won't hurt them, I guess,' Trent said, feeding a cube of sugar to his horse.

'If you treated your women as well as that horse,' Howie said, 'you'd have company in the sack tonight.'

Trent gestured and swore.

'No sharing the bedroll tonight, Howie,' Molly admonished. 'We can rest up properly once we're on the other side of the mountain.'

Beyond, its dark huge shape against the night sky above the treetops, Grim Mountain loomed.

Clint rode Beatrice past the trees and foliage and into a clearing. If his memory served him well, and his estimation of direction and time were reasonably accurate, he knew this place.

His heart hammered in sudden fear. He was a sitting duck here! They were in plain view in front of a shack where he'd stayed overnight a few times. He smelled the old wood and dew-damp mud.

He hauled back on the donkey's reins.

Something was wrong, he knew. Mutt was making a strange plaintive sound in his throat. Not a bark. Unlikely to be a threat, then. His hand hovered over the butt of his Dragoon. But his ears detected no unnatural sound. Whatever was upsetting Mutt, he felt sure that it had nothing to do with anybody lying in wait at the shack. He'd bet his life on there being no other human being anywhere near. He fleetingly smiled. At one time, he'd have bet on which leaf a fly would land. Whoever was with Belle, they'd been and gone, taking her with them.

Clint slid off Beatrice's back and unfastened the rope from the saddle and let Mutt lead him over rocky ground. Gradually, he shortened the length of lead until Mutt was only a couple of feet ahead of him. By then, he estimated that they were standing quite near the porch of the shack.

Mutt moved to the left and sniffed the air, then he moved to the right and paced to and fro. Clint reckoned the animal was confused somehow, as if torn between two opposing scent trails, which didn't make sense at all. Abruptly, Mutt stopped in his tracks, facing to the right and let out a yap of recognition and wagged his tail.

Clint tied his dog to a porch post then knelt down and carefully examined the ground with his fingertips. No mistaking the signs – three horses moved north, while two horses and the buckboard wheels headed south. He didn't bother going inside the shack. If Belle had been in there, Mutt would have rushed in and found her. It was obvious, the stronger scent caught by Mutt seemed to be to the right, in the northerly direction.

Hope rose in his chest. He guessed they were gaining on Belle and her abductors, since Mutt seemed to be straining at his rope leash.

When he heard unusual sounds over to the left, he reined in Beatrice and swiftly, silently slipped off the animal's back.

Definitely voices and the occasional clang of metal.

'Quiet, Mutt, there's a good dog,' he ordered and soundlessly led the donkey off the road and down a slight rough incline. He moved a few paces till his cane touched

the bole of a tree, then another. They'd afford concealment from the trail. He tethered Beatrice to a tree and
fumbled in his pack, replacing his boots with moccasins.

He untied Mutt from Beatrice and knelt beside the dog.
'Not a sound, old boy, understand?'

Mutt let out a slow guttural noise, more like a whisper.

Slowly, one hand on a shortened leash, the other
waving the cane in front of him, Clint moved into the
forest. His heart pounded. He felt vulnerable, not being
able to see anything or anybody. If someone heard him, he
was a goner. Already, he smelled the fresh water of the
creek. High above, zephyrs played in the topmost
branches of the trees. Boxtree and elder, if he remembered right.

His pulse raced in anticipation. But his body belied that
hope. It seemed as if every pore exuded sweat. What could
he do, since he was blind? Sure, the darkness was his ally,
and he was familiar with the terrain. But any wild shots –
even his own – might kill Belle.

Clearwater Creek rippled up ahead and to his left.
Worry about the confrontation when it was inevitable, he
told himself. He hauled on Mutt's leash and hunkered
down to listen for clues.

Voices of three people about twenty or twenty-five feet
away, he'd guess, muffled by the foliage between. Slowly,
he slunk over the forest floor, careful how he distributed
his weight. His old tracking sense had returned: he felt the
brush and deadwood through the soles of his moccasins.
Any spring or resistance warned of a twig about to snap, in
which case he lifted his foot and moved it slightly to one
side for more firm ground.

He estimated he'd covered a good ten feet and was
close. Now he could make out what was being said. Two

men and a woman, but, by God, her voice wasn't Belle's.

Clint waylaid an intake of breath before he made a sound. He shut one eyelid, then the other to be sure, and his heart leapt just a little: his left eye detected a faint yellow shimmering just ahead. He couldn't be sure, but it seemed like three dark shapes moving in front of a fire.

Lowering his body to the forest floor, he elbowed closer, and listened, all the while keeping the vague firelight blocked by tree trunks. He settled down and waited, but there was no mention of Belle. Faintly, he heard Mutt scuffling to his right. Damn, he'd been so overcome by the discovery that even a faint amount of light had penetrated his eye, he'd forgotten about his dog. Cursing himself, Clint moved soundlessly over the ground on his elbows, praying that he was still hidden by foliage. He glanced over his shoulder – must be, he thought, the shimmer of the campfire was blocked out now. Unless he'd imagined that tantalizing glimpse of light in his darkness?

Their horses were over to the right of the campsite, whickering.

Clint smelled bourbon wafting from the camp.

His heart hammered as he stood and then moved among the horses, calming them. He listened for the slightest indication that he'd been discovered. As he ran his hands over the horses, he was surprised to learn they were all still saddled, complete with bedroll strapped behind the cantle. The lazy swine were more interested in guzzling their whiskey than taking care of their mounts.

Mutt made a faint gruff sound, and Yankee, Belle's horse, gave Clint a familiar welcoming nudge. Then he found Taffy, his palomino: 'Yes, good to see you too feller.' He grinned at his choice of words.

With ghostlike tread, he shifted among the five horses

and whispered in turn: 'Easy, there. Quiet, there, quiet.'

One saddle-bag contained fabric, probably Belle's gingham dress, he reckoned. As he smelled her on the garment, his heart lurched – what have they done with her? Instinctively, he felt that she was not here in this camp, and clenched his hands into fists. Must control his anger. He was blind; if he went out among them, they'd gun him down and make sure this time. Clearly, Mutt had followed the scent of her dress. So where was she?

A single thought gave him hope: Mutt didn't find Belle's body on the trail. Surely, he would have traced her or any grave? This might explain Mutt's confusion at the shack; she'd gone south, not north.

Listening all the while, he checked the other horses, and inside the saddle-bags he found bundles of money. He didn't have to see it to know it: money gave off its own odour. He had no doubt the money was ill gotten. These people were desperate. They're not going to baulk at killing him to keep their loot.

Not being able to see, he'd already learned that it was so easy to lapse into a world of his own, divorced from reality, so that anything going on around him was cut off. Now he gave a start as the woman's voice got closer. She was walking over to the horses.

'Hey, Molly, don't bother bringing my bedroll – we can share!'

She laughed. 'Calm down, Howie! For now, I'm all tuckered out and just want to turn in and dream of what I'll do with my money.'

'Just keep your hands off of the saddle-bags!' shouted Howie.

'Temper, temper, just because I choose to sleep alone.'

'Tough luck, Howie,' said Trent.

This was them, all right; he recognized the names and the men's voices. Clint gritted his teeth and removed the hammer thong from his revolver. He backed away from the horses, soundlessly shifting branches aside, and waited in concealment.

Clint couldn't see Molly, but he heard her approach. She stopped at the horses and unbuckled her bedroll from the horse next to Yankee. Straight ahead, no obstructions. Without making a sound, Clint lunged. He'd guessed the distance well. His hand landed on her shoulder and before she could utter a word he swung the Dragoon butt down on her head. She slumped but he caught her. Her horse scuffled slightly then was still. He fingered her neck; a faint pulse, but she was definitely unconscious.

He heaved Molly's comatose body over the saddle of her horse. Now he gathered all the reins and used his Bowie knife to slit the hobbles securing their front legs.

And he led the horses away from the campsite. Mutt trailed beside them.

He smiled, thinking of his Crow friends of some years back, when he'd lived with them for about six months. They'd be mightily amused and proud of him, since they considered infiltrating an enemy camp and sneaking off with their horses was the true sign of a warrior. Not that his limping leg and hammering headache made him feel like a warrior.

The ground underfoot gradually sloped ahead and became rocky. He felt sure that this area was familiar. After they'd covered a few hundred feet, he halted the horses and separated Taffy and Yankee from the others. He recalled that there was plenty of grass in the area; they chewed contentedly while he transferred all the money into a single saddle-bag.

He dragged Molly off her horse and slapped its flank. It ran off with the other two, leaving him with the comatose outlaw woman, Mutt, Taffy and Yankee. With any luck, he'd collect Beatrice tomorrow.

He hefted Molly on to Yankee's saddle and tied her securely, then he took the reins of the two horses. 'OK, Mutt, find the cave,' he commanded.

Obediently, the dog scrambled ahead, further up a steep slope of jumbled rocks. Clint stumbled and banged his knees on outcrops a couple of times, which didn't do much for the wound in his thigh. Whenever he fell, he managed to retain his grip on the reins and they provided sufficient purchase and support most of the time.

Finally, the stones underfoot levelled out and he reckoned they'd reached the entrance to the cave.

He led the horses inside the cave, their hoofs echoing. He used strips off his buckskin tassels to hobble their front legs. 'We'll soon be home,' he whispered to Yankee and Taffy.

He released Molly from Yankee's saddle and lowered her to the ground. He cut strips off Mutt's rope leash and tied Molly's wrists and ankles. Then he used her bandana to blindfold her and waited with mixed emotions.

This woman was obviously the third member of the gang, the one responsible for his blind state. She'd also been instrumental in Belle's abduction. His normally strong respect for womankind was sorely tested as he sat and let time pass.

Eventually, he detected the sound of movement from her.

'Where – where am I?' Her voice echoed.

'Welcome back, Molly Nelson,' he said, his words

bouncing off the cave walls.

She jerked her head round. 'Who the hell are you, you coward! Where am I?'

'I'm justice, my dear. As for where you are, you're in your tomb – unless you start talking. . . .'

Howie and Trent spent a sleepless night, trying to find their horses. It was dawn when they finally located Howie's bay and Molly's chestnut grazing. The sorrel was nowhere to be seen.

The saddle-bags were empty; Trent flung them on the ground. 'Molly's run off with the loot!'

'Then why didn't she take her own horse?'

'It's obvious, isn't it? She's taken the Brennans' instead!'

His feet sore with the overnight search, Howie scoured the trail but to no avail. He was no good at tracking, never had been. He swore and mounted the chestnut. 'Which way'd the bitch go?'

'Not towards Rapid City, that's for sure.' Trent turned from tightening the bay's cinch and made a sweeping gesture. 'Maybe she'll double back through Bethesda?'

'Why'd she do that? It's a mite risky.'

Trent mounted the bay. 'Not really. The woman in the bank didn't see Molly, did she?'

'True enough. Damn, she's gone and used me!' Howie snapped.

'Us,' Trent corrected.

'Yeah.' Howie bit his lip and veered his mount towards the trail they'd travelled yesterday. 'Come on, let's hunt her down!'

CHAPTER SEVEN

MRS KILBRIDE

Wedlock seemed a larger town than Bethesda Falls, Belle thought, as Gamlin drove the buckboard along the wide main street. On their left was the livery and stage depot, an undertaker's parlour, a hurdy-gurdy house, the bank and sheriff's office; on the right, a general store, an eatery, a hotel, a barbershop and a church. Streets seemed to go back on each side, about four deep at least. People were busy opening their premises for a new day.

Gamlin stopped his buckboard outside the bank. 'I won't be long, Mrs Brennan,' he said.

'I'm not going anywhere.' She hugged her arms round her, feeling conspicuous with a horse blanket covering her legs and the plaid coat concealing her chemise.

'Do you want me to take your team to the livery, Mister?' asked a crippled man wearing a denim shirt and a Union forage cap. 'I'll be happy to oblige, sir!'

Irritably, Gamlin eyed the man. 'No, damnit, I don't. If I wanted the livery, I'd've stopped there first!'

'Just trying to make an honest living, sir.' His eyes were

like soot, his hair, moustache and beard grizzled.

Belle laid a hand on Gamlin's arm. 'Jeremy, please give the man something to tide him over. He looks like he could do with a good meal.'

Reluctantly, Gamlin said, 'Oh, very well.' He fished in his waistcoat pocket and flung a few coins to the ground. 'Here, but that's all you'll ever get from me!'

As the man bent with difficulty to retrieve the coins, Gamlin jumped down. He rummaged in the wagon bed behind the seat and extracted a large canvas bag.

Gamlin climbed the puncheon board steps and opened the bank door. Its bell tinkled.

The crippled man stood on the boardwalk and watched Gamlin go inside. 'I guess he's an important businessman and has no time for the likes of me.' He turned to leave.

'Wait!' Belle called.

Swivelling round in an awkward motion, the man said, 'Ma'am?' He briefly doffed his hat.

'I don't have any money with me at present,' Belle said, 'otherwise I'd have gladly accepted your offer of help. What kind of work do you do?'

'Charles Edward Pitman at your service, ma'am. I fought in the war, was in the artillery. Got good eyes but a game leg.' He brushed a hand over the dusty knees of his denim britches. 'I can try my hand at almost any kind of work, ma'am. I can be found at Ma Nicholson's boarding house.'

'Thank you, Mr Pitman. I may require someone to accompany me back to Bethesda Falls. Would you be interested?'

'Surely would, ma'am.'

'Good. Once I've made arrangements, I'll send word. Probably tomorrow.'

*

Gamlin shrugged off the slight distraction of the crippled beggar and strode purposefully into the bank. The bell clanged as he shut the door. At the far end of the room was the counter, its serving grille and a bank teller; on the right of the door, under the window, the bank manager sat, his desk plaque stating *Mr Reece Walsh.*

'Mr Walsh, how are you today?'

'Ah, Mr Gamlin. Good to have you back.' Walsh stood and brushed tobacco off his dark grey frock coat. A pipe smouldered in his left hand. He was about forty, fair-haired and blue-eyed, with a pasty complexion. They shook hands.

Walsh peered over the top of his wired eyeglasses, out the window. 'Is that your wife-to-be?'

'Wife?'

'Mrs Kilbride said you'd be returning with a new wife, sir.'

Gamlin smiled ruefully. 'Mrs Kilbride is mistaken. She's a bit romantic. Have you got your realtor's hat on, Mr Walsh?'

'For you, Mr Gamlin, of course.'

Gamlin opened the bag and dumped a bundle of bills on the desk. 'Here's the final payment for the property.'

Walsh sat down and leant over. He scooped the bundle towards him. 'Mrs Kilbride should have the place all cleaned up for you by now, I shouldn't wonder,' he said, swiftly counting the money.

'Good. It's very trusting of you to let us take possession before I'd liquidised my assets.'

The bank manager's face took on a smug look. 'I'm a good judge of character, Mr Gamlin.'

'Nice of you to say so.'

'Besides, your down-payment was generous.' Walsh scrawled a receipt from a pad and handed it to Gamlin. 'Fully paid. I'll get the papers sent over to you tomorrow.'

'Excellent. Now, I'd like to deposit $4,000,' Gamlin said, pulling out more money.

'Of course.'

This time, before Walsh could scoop it away, Gamlin covered the bills with a hand. 'I hope it'll be safe? I mean, the bank at Bethesda Falls was recently robbed.'

'Your money is safe here, sir, I can assure you. Safe as houses.'

The house stood at the end of town, on a slight slope. It was big, Belle thought, as the wagon drove between the two gate pillars. It had pointed windows and doorways, sharply gabled roofs, and two tall round towers with windows. The drive curved towards a set of imposing stone entrance steps and a portico complete with Doric pillars. She glanced at Gamlin.

'It's mine, in the gothic revival style,' he said, pushing out his chest. 'Just put down the final payment on it.'

She wondered how he'd been able to afford it.

Her face must have betrayed her thoughts because he shrugged, indifferent. 'Inheritance from a relative, he hit it big in California. . . .'

'It's a magnificent house.'

'I'm glad you like it.'

'You've been most fortunate in your luck, Mr Gamlin.'

'So I have. Though I tend to say, you make your own luck.' He faced her. 'Why don't you stay here a while? It'll give you time to mourn. Separate rooms, of course.'

'Of course,' she said.

'Is that "of course you'll stay"?'

She shook her head. 'No, it meant I'd expect our rooms to be separate, especially since I'm a new – if somewhat pecuniary – widow.'

'Of course. Let me help you down.'

Clutching the blanket around her midriff, Belle let him assist her. She then ascended the porch steps with some difficulty.

'Also,' he said, 'we're blessed with Mrs Kilbride, the family nurse, housekeeper, and confidante, to look after our needs.'

As if summoned by his words, a tall slim woman opened the front door and stepped on to the porch.

'Mrs Kilbride,' he said, 'this is Mrs Brennan. She's recently become a widow.'

'I'm so sorry to hear of your loss, ma'am,' said Mrs Kilbride. Her hair was tarnished sunset, her piercing eyes of jade. Her complexion was lily-white, emphasised by the deep dark green of her leg-o-mutton sleeved blouse and linen skirt complete with bustle.

'Th-thank you,' said Belle.

Gamlin gently shoved Belle in through the doorway. 'She'll take care of you. She's been looking after me for years!'

'Welcome home, sir,' said Mrs Kilbride as she closed the door after them.

'Thank you, Mrs Kilbride.'

'What happened to your head, Master Gamlin?' she asked, concern in her deep voice.

'Oh, no need to fuss, Mrs Kilbride, it's nothing, just a scratch.'

'Very well, sir.' The housekeeper turned to Belle. 'This way to your room, ma'am.' She gave Belle a studied glance. 'I think there may be some clothes that will fit you in the wardrobe.'

'Thank you,' Belle said, climbing the wide carpeted stairs behind the housekeeper.

Above, on the ornately balustraded landing, doors led off to various rooms.

Mrs Kilbride indicated the door at the head of the staircase. 'This is Mr Gamlin's room.' She turned to the right. 'Follow me, please, your room is the third one along.'

She swung open the big oak door to reveal a large bedroom, the walls covered in gold and red striped flock. Matching curtains flanked the two windows. The large metal bedstead was made up with white linen. On the left, a mantelpiece and hearth, an empty fireplace adorned with a potted plant, plus a tallboy with six drawers; on the right, a ceiling-high wardrobe, its door inlaid with a full-size mirror.

Easing open the wardrobe door, Mrs Kilbride ran her hand over a number of colourful garments hanging from rails. 'I'd recommend the dark blue dress, ma'am.'

'There seem to be a lot of blue ones.'

Mrs Kilbride shrugged. 'It will suit your complexion perfectly.' She swung round, raised her left eyebrow. 'You like duck, do you?'

'Duck?'

'To eat at supper—'

'Oh, yes, well no, I haven't had any for an age. I do like it, though.'

'Good. You *will* be coming down for supper, I hope? We have much to discuss.'

'Discuss?' Belle shook her head. 'I'm sorry, I'm still a bit shaken. Discuss what, Mrs Kilbride?'

Belle didn't get an answer. 'I can see you're tired after

your journey, Mrs Brennan.'

The housekeeper moved to the door. 'I'll leave you to get refreshed and changed and drop in to take you down to supper at seven.' She nodded at an ormolu clock on the mantelshelf. It was five now.

Belle wore the blue dress. She was sure she detected some brief but strange emotion in Mr Gamlin's eyes as she stepped off the bottom stair. If she hadn't known better, she'd have sworn he'd seen a ghost. He recovered quickly, however and led her through the double doors into the dining room.

The big mahogany table was set for two. Mrs Kilbride stood to one side, by the matching cupboard, its surface filled with desserts, fine china and wine decanters. Indeed, Mr Gamlin had been most fortunate.

During the meal – 'I think you'll like the wild duck, it was marinated in wine then fried' – Gamlin reluctantly talked about Clint, the secret gambling, the debts.

Tears filled Belle's eyes and Mrs Kilbride kindly stepped over to take her hand. 'Here, my dear, have another drink,' she said and refilled Belle's glass with red wine.

'I can't believe it,' Belle said. She sipped the wine, swallowed. 'There must be some mistake. Clint vowed gambling was in his past. . . .'

Gamlin shook his head. 'I'm sure his intentions were good, but once the bug bites, it's hard to shake off, or so I hear.'

'But the homestead and land, it was our future. We staked everything on it.' She shook her head. 'He wouldn't jeopardize all that.'

'I'm sorry, really sorry,' Gamlin said. 'I wish I hadn't been the one to tell you.'

Belle wiped her eyes. 'No, it's good of you. I mean, if it wasn't for your brave intervention, I'd probably be sold somewhere as – as. . . .' She felt a little faint.

'Would you like a slice of apple spice cake?' he asked, poised to cut into it.

Belle shook her head. 'It looks very nice, but I'm not feeling too well.' She tried to stand but her legs seemed incapable of supporting her.

'There, there, my dear.' Mrs Kilbride rushed to Belle's side, took her arm. 'Sir, I think Mrs Brennan should go up to her room and rest. She's had a distressful time of it, from what you've told me.'

'Yes, of course, Mrs Kilbride.' He stood, easing his chair back. 'It's most discourteous of me.' He dabbed his napkin at his mouth and his storm sea eyes levelled on hers. 'I hope you'll feel a little better on the morrow, ma'am.'

'Thank you for your kindness, Mr Gamlin.' A little awkwardly, she stood and left with the firm support of Mrs Kilbride on her arm.

Life was a balancing act and in her trade Grace Tabor had to do things she'd rather not. This was one of those occasions. She sat opposite Mayor Coop Pringle in her private dining room. Grace poured red wine from a Waterford Crystal decanter. In the centre of the table was a plate of pumpkin cheesecake. An ornate vase of sweet blossom flowers lent their fragrance to the room. It helped dispel the mayor's body odour. His voice was syrupy, which got him the votes, but invariably his words were insincere. 'Always say the Bella Union brings class to our town, Miss Grace.' He lowered his knife and fork on the bony remains of the quail in beer.

'Kind of you to say so, Coop. Though I can guess you

don't offer that observation to your good wife?'

He leaned back in his chair; he seemed unsure where to place his elbows. 'Well, no, she's a bit of a sensitive disposition, you realize.'

'What reason do you have to call on me? I don't recollect having you here in almost two years. Mrs Pringle is all right in that department, I hope?'

He nodded vigorously, colour tainting his sallow complexion. 'Oh, yes, she's fine, fine. I just need to take my mind off of the robbery. Mighty worrying time.' He wiped his forehead with the white napkin.

'Won't you be missed?'

'No, I'm "out of town on business". . . . You know. . . .'

She smiled and raised her wineglass. 'Why, that's most inventive of you, Coop. I'm sure few husbands have thought of that excuse.'

His cobalt eyes lanced hers. 'You're making fun of me, Miss Grace.'

'I wouldn't dream of it, Coop.' She lowered her voice. 'I hesitate to broach the subject, but my rate has increased since we last . . . you know. . . ? Funds are difficult since my partner absconded with the contents of the Union's safe.'

'What, Molly Nelson?'

'Yes, the little bitch.'

'She robbed you?'

'Yes, and after we'd been such good pals. I foolishly trusted her. We both sank all we had in this here parlour house. Then she just up and went – the same day as the bank robbery.'

He pulled a face. 'Don't remind me. A terrible day, that, one of the worst in my life. Poor Miss Wilson's been confined to her bed since the sorry episode. What with Gamlin resigning and her unable to work, Eustace says he's short-staffed.'

'Well, since he doesn't have much money left in the bank to look after, that's not so bad, is it?'

Pringle let out a hoop of a laugh. 'That might be funny, Miss Grace, but not to me it ain't. I don't know what the world's coming to, I really don't.'

'Too right, there's little honesty left, if you ask me. So you see, although it's against my better nature, I really must ask for your payment in advance. . . .'

He hesitated. 'I understand.' He lifted his napkin to the table and retrieved his billfold from the black coat's inside pocket.

He paused as they heard a commotion outside in the main street. They both got up from the table and moved to the window.

Trailing dust, the posse entered town. Some of the horsemen swerved off to the livery opposite, others rode on to the sheriff's office halfway up Main Street.

The Mayor's face paled. 'I don't see any strangers – villains under arrest. . . .'

'Maybe they shot the robbers. With any luck!'

'Maybe. . . .' He glanced down at her. 'I'm sorry, I'd better go and see what Deputy Johnson's got to say for himself.' He hesitated at the door, guilt written all over his face.

'Go out the back door, Coop – it's still there – to protect your image.'

'Thanks, Miss Grace. Very considerate.'

'Like old times, eh?'

He nodded. 'I'm sorry to – well, you know. . . .'

'The regret is all mine, Mayor,' she cooed and he was gone.

Grace bit her lip. She'd spent a pretty penny on this

meal, and it was all wasted. Mayor Pringle left with his bill-fold unopened. Damn the posse's lousy timing!

Belle awoke on top of the bed-covers and felt disoriented. She was still dressed. An oil lamp flickered on the bedside table. Her bare arms raised goose bumps; she was chilled, which wasn't surprising since the clock said it was three in the morning. Her head ached, voices ringing in her mind, but she couldn't remember what kind of voices. But she'd only had a glass of wine – or was it two? Perhaps it was a little too rich for her taste.

She swung her legs off the bed and crossed over to the door, but it was locked. She moved to the window and pulled the curtain back; but the sash was screwed down. Quite irrational, she told herself, but she felt like a prisoner.

Then she noticed the cream silk nightgown draped over a wicker chair, and a washbasin and jug on a table. Prisoner? Nonsense.

She poured tepid water from the jug and cupped her hands to wash her face. It helped refresh her a little.

That dizzy spell at supper was worrying, but rest was probably the answer. She'd get ready for bed and sleep. The prospect seemed very attractive. She undressed slowly, hardly able to keep her eyes open, and finally drew back the bedcovers. No sooner had she flopped on to the bed, pulled the covers over her and rested her head on the pillow, than she was asleep.

About an hour later, Gamlin unlocked the door and entered her bedroom. He was in his shirtsleeves. Tiptoeing over the carpet, he reached the wicker chair. He sat and proceeded to study Belle.

His eyes were red rimmed and a vein in his temple pulsed.

Some time afterwards, he stirred himself and moved to the bedside. He brushed away stray locks of Belle's auburn hair and pulled out from his pants pocket a pair of scissors.

CHAPTER EIGHT

MEAN BUSINESS

The barber's scissors snipped firmly at the black moustache under Howie's crooked nose. Then the small clumps of hair were brushed away to join Trent's shorn blond locks on the floor. He was sorry to see it go.

The entrance door was open, its glass panel labelled, *C Wilcox, Barber, Dentist & Undertaker.*

Chauncey Wilcox, the Barber and Undertaker stropped his razor then smartly shaved the stubbly remains of Howie's moustache. 'That's taken ten years off of you, Mister,' he said.

'Thanks. I hear there was a bank raid the other day,' Howie said, boldly. He was amused to see in the mirror that Trent's burlap complexion paled.

'Aye,' said Chauncey, 'the first in this town – and the last, I reckon.'

'The last? Why's that?'

'The mayor's putting an armed guard on the bank in future.' Chauncey used a fine brush to wipe away hairs around Howie's ears. 'Nobody gets in wearing guns.'

'Armed guard – that'll be expensive.'

'Aye, well they haven't got any money in the bank at the moment. But they're scouting around for suitable recruits. Judging by the way your rigs sit on you, maybe that's the kind of work you two gents'd be interested in?'

'Maybe.' Howie stopped talking as he noticed the reflection in the mirror: two men, one portly, one tall, stopped in the open doorway.

'Be with you in a minute, Mr Hayes, Mr Mayor,' said Chauncey.

'Take your time, Mr Wilcox.'

'Well, as I was saying,' Howie resumed, 'we were just passing through. Thought we'd pay a visit to the Bella Union – that's why we're getting spruced up.'

'If you two gents want the job,' said Hayes, 'I reckon I could get the town council to hire you.'

With a flourish, Chauncey removed the hair-laden cape. Howie stepped out of the chair and the barber brushed down Howie's black shirt.

'Sounds interesting,' Howie said. 'Are you the mayor or Mr Hayes?'

Hayes straightened up, thrusting his shoulders back, so his belly became more pronounced. 'I'm the aggrieved bank manager, sir. Who am I addressing?'

'I'm Rutherford,' Howie said, 'and this is my partner, Dullard.'

'Are those surnames?' the mayor asked.

'The only names we go by,' explained Howie. Before entering town, Howie had discussed what alias to use. He was convinced they hadn't spoken their names in the bank, but to play safe they'd go by surnames only.

'I see.' Hayes eyed their six-guns, glanced at the mayor and nodded.

96

At that moment, a woman walked past the barber's window then stopped. 'Ah, there you are, Mr Hayes!'

Howie's blood ran cold all the way down his spine.

Hayes turned, doffed his hat. 'Miss Wilson, are you all right? I thought you'd still be resting up.'

'Oh, I couldn't stay shut away, sir. Must get on with life. Can't be hiding away.'

'That's mighty brave of you, ma'am,' said the mayor in his syrupy tone.

She flushed then glanced in through the doorway. 'Good morning, gentlemen. New to town?'

'Howdie, ma'am,' said Howie, his voice having adopted a deeper, more gruff tone. 'Yes, Ma'am. And a nice town it is, too.' He counted out coins in Chauncey's outthrust palm.

'So it is, sir.' She turned back to Hayes. 'When would you like me to start work again, sir?'

'Tomorrow would be fine, Miss Wilson. And thank you for your loyalty.'

'My pleasure. Good day, gentlemen, Mr Mayor.' She strode off.

Howie let out a faint sigh of relief and he and Trent retrieved their sombreros from the horn-rack.

As the four of them strolled along the boardwalk, Hayes asked, 'Did you say something about visiting the Bella Union?'

Howie nodded, putting his hat on; it was a loose fit now. 'A pal told me to look up a gal called Molly Nelson, said she works there.'

'Used to,' said the mayor. 'She lit out with the takings. The owner. . . .' He stopped as Deputy Johnson approached from behind them.

Again, Howie's heart did a slick somersault. First Miss

Wilson, now it's the law!'

'I didn't know about that,' said Johnson.

'Me neither,' said Hayes, looking at Mayor Pringle strangely.

'No?' said the mayor. 'Maybe it slipped Miss Tabor's mind.'

'When did she tell you, Mayor?' Hayes asked.

'I got it third hand, I think.' He seemed flustered, not the suave self-possessed man who earlier greeted Miss Wilson.

'Oh, well, I'm sure there'll be plenty of other nice gals to visit while we're here,' said Howie. 'Now, about our wages for this security job. . . .'

'See Mr Hayes,' said the mayor. 'It's his bank they robbed.'

'OK. Can we board somewheres, then come calling on you, Mr Hayes?'

'Certainly. I'd recommend The Constitution Hotel – back the way you've come, next to the barber's in fact.'

'He's got shares in it,' said Mayor Pringle.

'Thank you kindly, gentlemen,' said Howie. He tipped a finger to his hat. 'Excuse us.' He turned on his heel and walked back along the boardwalk with Trent at his side.

Mayor Pringle eyed Deputy Johnson. 'They look mean, Deputy.'

'And they mean business, I reckon,' said Hayes.

Johnson shrugged. 'It's your money, Mr Hayes. While the mayor selects the sheriff and deputies, it's your town rates that pay my wages. I'll continue to do my job the best I can, but if you want to hire extra help, that's your privilege. So long as they stay within the law.'

*

Next morning, Belle woke with the sun streaming into the bedroom. Mrs Kilbride stood at the foot of the bed holding a tray of breakfast: waffles, scrambled egg, syrup and coffee.

'Did you sleep well, Mrs Brennan?'

'Yes, thank you. I'm sorry about last night, I must have been very tired.'

'You've been under considerable strain, it's only to be expected.'

Mrs Kilbride placed the tray in front of her and Belle tucked in. 'I'm ravenous,' she said.

Hands clasped sedately in front of her, Mrs Kilbride looked on approvingly.

'Tell me,' Belle said, licking some syrup from the side of her mouth. 'I'm curious, how did you know that dress and this nightgown would fit me?'

'I have a good eye for measuring up people, Mrs Brennan. I think I have your measure exactly.'

'But—'

'The clothes belonged to Mr Gamlin's late wife, Lydia. She died a few years back but he couldn't bear to part with them, so I ensure they're kept in good condition.'

'Oh, I'm sorry to hear that.' A slight shiver ran through her and she suddenly felt uncomfortable, wearing a dead woman's clothing.

'I assure you, all her clothes have been cleaned and preserved. You won't find the slightest hint of camphor.'

'Yes – and the blue dress too?'

'Of course. Would you like to wear it again today?'

'It isn't too formal for day-wear?'

'Mrs Brennan, it suits you and it isn't as though you have any chores to do about the house. That is my job.'

'Chores. . . . Our home. . . .' Belle felt tears fill her eyes.

She laid the tray to one side and swung her legs out of bed. 'I really must go back and take care of things.'

Mrs Kilbride strode forward, hands clasped in front of her bosom. 'Mr Gamlin has already done that. He telegraphed the Deputy Sheriff at Bethesda Falls and he and Dr Strang are probably already there to see to… your poor husband.'

Belle clasped a hand to her chest and felt a surge of relief. 'Thank you.'

'Anything else, Mrs Brennan?'

'Can you leave me while I get dressed?' And devote her thoughts to Clint.

'Yes, of course.'

As she washed and dressed, Belle couldn't get rid of a feeling of guilt. Was this the second or third morning she'd awoken without Clint by her side? She should be grieving, not parading around in a dead woman's dress, not eating wild duck and drinking rich wine. What was the matter with her? Clint deserved more than this. It was as if he was merely an afterthought.

Then those voices again. Vague, whispering, insistent, as if haunting her. What was all that about? A bad dream, sure, but why? Stay clear of the wine, she admonished herself.

Later, wearing the blue dress, Belle descended the stairs and glided towards the front door. But Mrs Kilbride waylaid her. 'That wouldn't be such a good idea, Mrs Brennan. The master doesn't want you to leave. It's for your own good.'

Surprised and taken aback by Mrs Kilbride's tone, Belle snapped, 'What am I supposed to do all day? Sit around?'

'I'm sure you can find something to do.'

'Mr Gamlin promised he'd make arrangements to get me back to Bethesda Falls.'

'I know he did. But you agreed he'd do that after his business was concluded in town.'

'What is his business?'

'Minding his own.'

Prickly, Belle thought and turned on her heel and climbed the stairs. Once on the landing, she glanced over the banister rail. Mrs Kilbride walked down the passage that led to the kitchen. Belle hesitated at Mr Gamlin's door. She tried the handle. It was unlocked. No reason to be otherwise, she supposed, since it was his home.

The room was well appointed – curtains and carpet – Mrs Kilbride's doing, obviously. A bit sombre, she thought; hardly any daylight percolated in here.

At least the room she'd occupied last night had been cheerful and possessed colour.

On Gamlin's bed was a grey suit, laid out as if ready to be worn.

She was drawn to the linen chest on the right and picked up a framed miniature painting of a woman. She let out a gasp and almost dropped it as she realized that the woman possessed features strongly resembling her own.

CHAPTER NINE

ASSASSINS FOR HIRE

Charles Edward Pitman leant against the porch post opposite the livery and watched the world go by, hoping to accost newcomers who'd trust him with their livestock. His eyes widened as he noticed a strange procession that entered town. Slowly, he hobbled down the steps.

A collie limped along on a lengthy leash, leading a horseman. The man's clothes were blood-spattered and his face was a mess. 'God almighty,' Pitman whispered, 'he's blind.' Blind he may be, but the man rode easy in the saddle, conveying strength of purpose and – something Pitman hadn't seen in a while – true grit. A cane slapped lightly at the side of the chestnut horse. Trailing behind was a palomino, and slung over its saddle was a body. No, it wasn't a corpse, as there was slight struggling movement. 'Well, I'll be damned.' He removed his forage cap and scratched his head. 'It's a woman.' Now he could see that she was blindfolded and gagged, her hands tied behind her back. Must be uncomfortable, he reckoned. And in the rear trotted a donkey.

Pitman stepped out in front of the rider.

The dog raised his hackles and barked.

'Easy, Mutt,' the man said, his voice deep and firm. 'What is it?' The rider hauled on the reins.

'Hey, Mister, if you're looking for help, I'm your man. Charles Edward Pitman. I fought in the war, was in the artillery. Got good eyes but a game leg.'

'Thanks for the offer, Mr Pitman.' He leaned down from his saddle and extended his hand. His face was a bloody mess. 'Brennan. Clint Brennan.'

He had a firm handshake.

'Have you seen a new wagon enter town in the last day or two? I've been tracking it.'

'Tracking? How. . . ?'

Clint indicated Mutt. 'He's as good as my eyes most times. But I'd appreciate it if you could help me as well, Mr Pitman.'

'Sure, Mr Brennan, but drop the "Mr". I was given the moniker Pits in the army and it's kinda stuck.'

'OK, Pits. Call me Clint. Now, about that wagon?'

'The only new wagon I've seen recently was a buck-board, come in yesterday. A nice lady and her sour gent. I don't know her name, but she called him Jeremy.'

Clint smiled. 'Thank you, Pits.' A few seconds of silence passed. 'Is there something else you'd like to tell me?'

'How'd you know?'

'Just a guess.'

'Well, the lady, she intended returning to Bethesda Falls as soon as she could make arrangements. Asked me to accompany her.'

'I see. But?'

'That was supposed to be today, but she hasn't sent word yet.'

'Maybe she will later. Now can you direct me to the sheriff's office, please?'

'I'll take you.'

'I'd appreciate that.'

Even in the outer office, they could hear Molly Nelson shouting profanities. 'I reckon as soon as you let women wear pants, they get as bad as men,' said Sheriff Terry Hopkins as he hung the jail keys on their hook next to the rifle case.

Clint refrained from replying; he'd heard worse from her in the cave. It had required a great test of his willpower, but he'd been reluctant to torture her, despite what she'd done to him. She'd readily admitted to robbing the bank – the evidence was in the saddle-bags, after all. As for her gang's raid on his ranch, all she'd admit was that she'd been hired to kill him. She wouldn't say by whom or why. 'Yeah, I'm sorry. Sorry I didn't check your corpse and put a slug in your skull.' Those words, even recalled now, sent a chill through him.

Hopkins sat at his desk. 'Take a seat, Mr Brennan.'

'Thanks.' Unerringly, Clint sank into the chair. Pitman stood to one side behind him and Mutt lay at Clint's feet.

'You look in a bad way,' said the sheriff. 'Those wounds need medical care. Where are you staying?'

Clint cocked his head at Pitman.

'I'll find him a room at the hotel, Sheriff.'

'And for yourself?' Clint said.

'I board at Ma Nicholson's,' Pitman said.

'Pits, I'd appreciate it if you'd take a room next to mine – until I've sorted out some unfinished business.'

104

'OK. I'll let Ma Nicholson know.'

'I'll send over Doc Trask,' the sheriff said. 'He's a good sawbones, he'll clean you up.'

'Thanks, I appreciate it.'

'Anything else?'

'Yes, Sheriff. Can you lock this in your safe till I leave?' He hefted a set of saddle-bags.

'Sure. I'll write out a receipt for you.'

Pitman signed the receipt as witness and Hopkins locked the safe.

'When I've done my rounds,' said Sheriff Hopkins. 'I'll drop in on the telegraph office and let Bethesda Falls know you'll be returning with their money and a felon.'

Clint raised a hand, troubled by some unfathomable instinct. 'No, wait a while. Give it a day. I might want to do a bit of investigating, if you have no objection, Sheriff?'

'No, no objection. I'm willing to help wherever I can, of course. But—'

'Mr Pitman here will be my eyes. I'm sure we'll manage. But if I need your help, I'll be sure to holler.'

They left the office, Clint taking faltering steps, Mutt on a short leash just ahead, Pitman limping by his side.

'Where to now?' asked Pitman.

'The hotel, as you suggested. Once we've got our rooms, we'll start asking around.'

'I reckon you need a change of clothes if you're going to be asking questions. Appearance counts, you know.'

The appearance of Clint Brennan in the main street of Wedlock shocked Gamlin to the core. He pulled back from the saloon window and watched as Brennan talked to that pest of a cripple. He bit his lip, removed his grey derby and wiped its inside band. If only he had the guts to face Brennan down. He glanced over his shoulder at the bar. Three roughshod men in their mid-twenties leant against the counter, feet on the brass rail, supping beer. The barkeep was at the far end; nobody else was in the saloon.

Gamlin called to the three men. 'Hey, gents, do you want to earn a little extra money?'

'Sure.' They left their drinks and sauntered over.

'I guess I better introduce myself. I'm Eustace Hayes,' Gamlin lied, 'and I'm tracking a man who murdered my wife.'

'That's a real shame, Mister.' They introduced themselves, first names only.

'What do you want doing?' asked Dave, the man with whiskers.

'See that man yonder?' He nodded out the window. 'The one in the buckskin jacket?'

The three men leaned to the pane then eyed Gamlin.

'Yeah,' said the pinch-faced man, Chad.

'He looks a mite unsteady on his feet,' said Ian, his features stern and thickset.

'So he does. . . . An easier target for you, then, isn't he?'

'Target, eh? When do you want rid of him?'

'Tonight would be good,' Gamlin suggested.

'How much are you willing to pay?' demanded Ian.

'Two hundred dollars. Each.'

Their eyes lit up.

'I'll give you one hundred now. The remainder when the deed's done.'

'You have a deal,' said Ian, clearly the spokesman.

Gamlin dipped inside his jacket and peeled off the bills, counted them out for each man.

They pocketed the notes, hitched their gun-belts and

106

strode out the saloon batwings.

Gamlin watched as the three men moved up the main street, a number of paces behind Clint Brennan and the crippled beggar.

CHAPTER TEN

EASY MONEY

Holding the small painting to her chest, Belle moved to Gamlin's bedroom window and looked out. Was this a picture of his wife? She felt uncomfortable; the resemblance wasn't an accident, she felt sure. The townspeople below went about their daily business, oblivious of her existence. She felt trapped and suddenly gasped.

Gamlin approached the porch of the house with almost a skip in his step. He was smiling.

She pulled back from the window and returned the picture to the linen chest. As she reached the door, she made up her mind. She left his room, closed the door behind her and stood on the landing, waiting.

She decided to demand that he fulfilled his promise to see her safely on her way back to Bethesda Falls.

The door opened into the tiled lobby and as if out of nowhere Mrs Kilbride glided to meet him. He handed her his grey derby, his lips peeled into a huge grin.

Holding her dress up so she wouldn't trip, Belle

descended the staircase. She cleared her throat. 'Mr Gamlin. . . .'

He turned to watch her. 'Jeremy, please.' His lips curved.

She smiled but she felt cold inside. 'Jeremy, you promised to see me on my way, back to Bethesda Falls. I must look to my dead husband.'

Gamlin flinched for a moment. 'Yes, your husband. . . . I know, and I'm a man of my word, Mrs Brennan. Didn't Mrs Kilbride tell you I've set things in motion for the poor man?'

'Yes, and I appreciate that,' she said, adding plaintively, 'but I should be there.'

'I agree, but unfortunately I'm deeply involved in a few serious business transactions. I've only returned for a change of clothes then I'll have to leave again. I'm so sorry.' He turned from her. 'Mrs Kilbride?'

'Yes, sir?'

'Is my grey suit ready?'

'Yes, sir, waiting on the bed.'

He left the two women standing in the lobby and raced up the stairs.

Belle stared after him, her throat dry.

Mrs Kilbride touched Belle's arm. 'Please, come into the kitchen and have a drink. Then I'll hitch up the buckboard and arrange for somebody to take you back to Bethesda.'

Belle's heart lifted and she smiled. 'Oh, thank you so much, Mrs Kilbride.'

Over coffee, Belle talked about Clint, their dreams and hopes, and she was unable to stop the tears. 'I'm sorry, but I don't feel I've even begun to mourn him yet.' She pressed a fist against her breast. 'It hurts so, this emptiness. . . .'

Mrs Kilbride put an arm round Belle's shoulders. 'There, there. . . .'

'Oh, dear, I feel dizzy, like last night. . . .'

'I think you have probably contracted a fever, Mrs Brennan. Let's take you up to bed and I'll go and arrange for the doctor to call on you.'

'But the buckboard. . . ?'

'It isn't going anywhere. Once the doctor has given you a clean bill of health, you can be on your way.'

'You're too kind, Mrs Kilbride.'

'Yes, they all say that.' Mrs Kilbride smiled.

Doc Trask was in his late thirties, Belle reckoned, and prematurely grey. He had kindly slate eyes, a prominent nose, and a reassuring manner. He sat on the bed at Belle's side and felt her pulse.

He nodded. 'A bit fluttery. Out of sorts, I suspect, ma'am. Nothing serious. Mrs Kilbride is quite right. The dizziness is probably due to delayed shock. My commiserations on your recent loss, Mrs Brennan.'

'Thank you, Doctor. But what about the "voices" I've heard? I'm not losing my mind, am I?'

He smiled. 'No, I believe it is merely a mild hallucination brought on by your change in circumstances. It will pass, given time. Certainly nothing to worry about.'

She nodded and forced a smile. The 'voices' were the most worrying aspect of her ailment. 'Would I be able to travel by wagon to Bethesda Falls this afternoon?'

He shook his head. 'No, I'd recommend complete rest for a day or so. Then you'll be fit enough to travel.' He looked up at the attentive housekeeper. 'I'm sure Mrs Kilbride will take good care of you.'

'Oh, she does, Doctor. Thank you again,' said Belle,

unable to conceal the disappointment in her voice.

'Don't worry, this phase will soon pass, I can assure you.' He stood. 'Mrs Kilbride, let's leave our patient to her rest.'

True to his word, Sheriff Hopkins had sent Doc Trask over to the hotel. By the bedside was a china bowl with a blood-soaked flannel and blood-tinted water. The room smelled of iodine.

'You're remarkably fit, Mr Brennan,' said Dr Trask, folding away his stethoscope.

'Apart from being blind and with a wounded leg.'

'That's nothing to do with your health.'

'No, I suppose not.' Clint stood and slipped on a grey shirt Pitman had bought from the General Store. It was a good fit, since the storekeeper had used Clint's old shirt and pants to make a comparison.

'I don't wish to sound ungrateful, Doc. Thanks for cleaning up my eyes. I feel better now I'm rid of all that dried blood.'

'I'm only sorry I can't do more for you. I'm no expert, Mr Brennan, but I reckon your right eye's definitely a goner. As for your left – you say you've glimpsed the odd light?'

'Difficult to say, Doc. Faint but definitely something there.' He explained about the campfire and the silhouettes.

Dr Trask sighed. 'It's an unusual case. From your description, it's what we call tunnel vision. I've known that to be caused by head injuries . . . whether permanent or not in your case, it's hard to say. Perhaps some specialist back East could examine and advise you. Some sufferers find their peripheral sight restored. Maybe you'll recover some sight in time.' He shrugged. 'The body heals itself.'

Clint grinned. 'I thought that's what you did, Doc, heal people?'

'Oh, I mend the obvious problems – set broken bones and treat gunshot wounds, but mostly I'm just the body's assistant. The body does most of the work, if it's a mind to.'

'If only. . . .' Clint mused.

'I must say, you've accepted your blindness with surprising calm. I – well, I'll be damned—' He paused and Clint detected it.

'What's the matter?'

'Sometimes I wonder if I'm getting senile before my time!'

'Senile? Why?'

'Where are you from, Mr Brennan?'

'A homestead just outside Bethesda Falls. Why?'

'Bethesda Falls, eh?'

'Do you mind telling me what all this is about, Doc?'

At that moment, Pitman entered the room. 'I've got a table booked in the restaurant, Clint. Once we've eaten, we can start asking those questions.'

'Fine, I must admit I'm hungry. Then we can be on our way.'

Dr Trask rested a hand on Clint's shoulder. 'You're not going out, surely?'

'I must,' said Clint.

'Your leg. . . .'

'Will have to heal itself in its own good time, won't it, Doc? Now, what's your interest in Bethesda Falls?'

'I honestly don't know what to make of it, but I've just come from a house where a Mrs Brennan is mourning the loss of her husband and is anxious to return to Bethesda Falls.'

*

Four men sat over the remains of rabbit stew in the hotel restaurant: the sheriff, the doctor, Pitman and Clint. Each smoked a cigar while they talked.

'Look, sheriff,' said Dr Trask, 'if I thought Mrs Brennan was being held against her will, I'd tell you.'

'Yes, I know.'

'By all accounts,' said Pitman, 'that residence used to belong to an eccentric Englishman.'

'So?' said the sheriff.

'So maybe people who live there become eccentric. Get changed by the house. That might explain it, huh?'

'You're not helping,' said Dr Trask. 'I can only repeat, the lady I attended fits the description Clint has given. Professionally, I can't divulge more, save that she is not seriously unwell. How do you wish to resolve this, Sheriff?'

'I could walk up to the front door and ask to speak to Mrs Brennan. Then I could question her.'

'Question her?' Clint queried.

'Remember, I've got a woman in my jailhouse who admits she's a bank robber and was hired to kill you. Don't take it the wrong way, but maybe your wife hired her. Maybe she's set up home with this guy Gamlin.'

Clint growled, 'I know you have to look at all angles, Sheriff, but you're dead wrong there.'

'Perhaps. But who else has a motive? Gamlin? Why'd he want rid of you?'

Clint shrugged. 'That has me puzzled. You know, I knew a Gamlin in Bethesda – the fellow worked in the bank.'

'Maybe a relation.'

'Could be.' Clint sighed. 'Time's passing, my wife is still in that house, and I'm real anxious to see – to make sure she's all right.'

'OK,' said Sheriff Hopkins. 'I reckon it'd be best if you

and me go on up to the Gamlin residence tonight – about eight o'clock. Less people about, more discreet.'

Clint said, 'Pits, how long till eight?'

'Three hours.'

'OK,' Clint said. 'I can wait that long, I guess.' He stood and Pits was by his side in an instant. 'I'll be in my room if there are any other developments.'

On their way up the staircase, Clint said, 'Do you carry a gun, Pits?'

'Used to, but I pawned it a few days back.'

Clint gave him some coins. 'Is that enough to get it back?'

'More than enough, I reckon.'

'Leave me in my room and then go get your gun. I have a feeling you might be needing it.'

'Sure, but I'm not much of a shot with it. Now if it was a cannon, I could hit a barn. Not sure I could hit one with my old Buntline.'

Clint chuckled. 'Any opposition doesn't know that, though.'

Mutt was pleased to see him return to his room. Clint dropped a couple of bones scrounged from the kitchen and the dog settled down with them.

Clint sank back on the bed, his emotions now a complete mess.

If Belle wasn't a captive in that house, why was she staying there? Why not? She thinks I'm dead, after all.

For a second or two it occurred to him to leave town. He knew she was alive and not in danger. That was enough. Let her mourn him in her own way. He was no good to her in his present state. She might as well move on, without him.

Exhaustion claimed him and he dozed.

The shadows lengthened and the room grew dark.

As the sash window slid open, it made a very faint squeaking sound. Chad's pinched face contorted, but there was no response from the man lying on the bed.

He cocked his Navy Colt.

A floorboard outside the room door groaned under Dave's weight.

They were ready. As soon as Dave busts open the door, Chad would fire at the man on the bed. Dave would shoot the dog. Ian stayed in the passage as extra backup.

Easy money.

CHAPTER ELEVEN

"DO YOUR WORST"

Clint's eyes opened at the first sound from the window. Total darkness. But his hearing and sense of smell seemed more attuned than ever and he detected a mixture of gun-oil and body odour on the breeze from the window.

Soundlessly, he slid out his Dragoon from under the pillow.

He heard a gun being cocked by the window.

Someone at the door as well.

Lying here, he was an obvious target.

Suddenly, the door was kicked and splintered loudly on its hinges.

Clint fired at the window and rolled off the bed. Glass splattered everywhere and a man screamed. The door clattered to the floor.

Mutt growled. Clint rose on one knee and fired at a vague human shape in the centre of the faintly lit quadrangle of light in the doorway.

Another scream, from the doorway, then a shot was fired.

'Hell, get the damned varmint off me!'

'Stand still, Dave, so I can get a clear shot!' Another voice, in the passage.

Suddenly, down the passageway Pitman called out, 'Drop your weapon!'

More shouts, and gunfire.

Clint knelt, listening, his one eye straining but seeing nothing.

Nearby scuffling and growling told him that Mutt still gripped one of the intruder's arms in his jaws.

Clint listened for any sound at the window.

'Hey, Chad, don't leave me!' shouted the man in Mutt's grip.

'We'll get the boys to break you out, have no fear!' called the man at the window. Clint heard him slither down the porch roof slates.

Above the sound of scuffling and growling, Pitman said from the doorway, 'I shot the second guy in the passage, but he ran off and exited through an open window and jumped. By the time I got there, he'd gone. Moved fast, even with a wounded leg,' he said, his tone almost envious. 'At least we've got this one, if your dog'll let him live.'

'Let go, Mutt!' Clint ordered and the dog snarled and moved to Clint's side. He patted his rump: 'Well done, boy.'

'I need a doctor, I've been shot!' Dave moaned. 'And look what your damned dog's done!'

'You'll be answering some questions, fella,' said Pitman. 'Either now, or when the sheriff gets here.'

'I've got nothing to say. It was a mistake, wrong room. I was after a man who robbed me at poker last week.'

'That's some story. I'll check with the barkeep. I must say, I can't imagine anyone, even a low down skunk like you, setting out to kill a blind man.'

'What're you talking about? What blind man?'

'See for yourself,' said Pitman.

Clint moved into the light of the open doorway.

'But you shot me!'

'Lucky, I guess.'

'Lucky nothing, that was a damned good shot,' said Pitman. 'You got his gun-arm.'

'I did?'

Dave was quiet a moment, as if studying Clint. 'Hell, I didn't know. . . .'

'A mistake, eh?' Pitman said with irony in his tone.

'Yes, sure it was. I wouldn't shoot a blind man, no way.'

'I see,' said Clint. 'But it's OK to shoot someone in his bed. Strange scruples you have, Mister.' He turned to Pitman. 'You know, Pits, I think my presence in this town has upset someone.'

At supper that evening, Belle again felt dizzy. 'Dr Trask says it must be the shock. I keep hearing voices, whenever I'm dozing.'

'Just bad dreams,' said Gamlin dismissively.

'No, it can't be, because I've woken from my dreams and I can still hear them, the voices.'

'Really?' He eyed Mrs Kilbride. 'What are these voices saying?'

She faltered. 'It's most awkward, Mr Gamlin.'

'Jeremy.'

'Well, Jeremy, the voices tell me to marry you!'

'Really? How strange – not that I don't consider you a most attractive and desirable woman. . . .'

'Please, don't be flippant, I'm worried. It's serious.'

'Sorry. Yes, as you say, it's most odd.'

'I've never experienced anything like this before.'

Gamlin shrugged, pointed at her with his fork. 'Perhaps some part of you seeks shelter, reassurance – even protection?'

'It seems a mite far-fetched to me.' She noticed a cloud pass over his face at her comment. She added, unsure. 'But I must admit, I do feel lost, cast adrift, since. . . .'

'Only natural,' he offered.

'But I wouldn't dream of seeking a new husband so soon, so soon after. . . .'

'I know. You're distraught, but perhaps deep inside you know what is best for your future. If you wish me to court you – after a suitable period, of course – I would consider it an honour.'

She flushed. 'It is most considerate of you, Jeremy. You have been too kind already. I can never repay you.' She gestured at her dress, the half-eaten food. 'You must miss your wife greatly.'

'Yes, she was a good friend and companion as well as the love of my life. Very much like you in looks, as it happens.'

She felt another wave of dizziness pass over her. Slowly, she nodded, unable to speak.

'Do think about it, won't you?'

'What?'

'Becoming my bride. . . .'

'That's very forward of you, Mr Gamlin – Jeremy. We've barely met – and I'm a – a new widow, still grieving. . . .'

Abruptly, Gamlin leaned across the table and grabbed Belle's wrist. 'Think before you reject me outright, my dear. I'm not a pleasant man when spurned.'

Mrs Kilbride stepped forward. 'Sir, you seem distraught. Is anything the matter?'

Gamlin let go of Belle.

'No, Mrs Kilbride. Everything is under control.' He eyed the clock. 'By now, I imagine everything has been sorted. . . .' He turned to Belle. 'I'm sorry, my dear. My little joke.'

'In poor taste, I fear.' Belle shuddered expressively, tears in her eyes. 'But you're right, of course. I have nothing to live for, now my husband's dead,' Belle responded, her head swaying as she fought off yet another dizzy attack. 'Do your worst, sir.'

'Oh, he will,' advised Mrs Kilbride.

CHAPTER TWELVE

'SO MUCH LOVE TO GIVE'

On the outskirts of the Missouri town of Carne Gulch, building renovations on an imposing residence were well underway. The new owners, a senator and his bride of six weeks, watched while picnicking.

It was a glorious day – until the normal noise of the builders abruptly ceased.

The site foreman ran up to the senator. 'You'd better come and see this, sir. No, leave your wife here.'

A false wall had been discovered and behind it was the corpse of a woman lying on a truckle bed. She wore a stained blue dress. Her long unkempt hair was auburn and her staring lifeless eyes still held a hint of blue-grey.

'Oh, my God!' said the senator, turning away. 'The poor woman.'

'I'm going to stop work till the marshal investigates this, sir.'

The senator nodded. 'Yes, I understand.'

121

Pitman hammered on the sheriff's office door till it was unlocked and opened. Bleary-eyed, Terry Hopkins said, 'What's up? It's not eight yet.' Then he noticed Dave clutching a bloody arm. 'You'd better come in.'

As the sheriff sat on the edge of his desk, Clint said, 'This man – calls himself Dave – and two others tried to shoot me in my bed a few minutes' ago.'

'I know him. Dave Rider, works for the Lazy-W.'

'It was all a mistake, Sheriff—'

'He says he was after a guy who cheated him at poker,' Clint said. 'We checked his alibi with the saloon barkeep; it doesn't hold up.'

'His arm seems in a bad way.'

'I shot him and my dog kept him out of mischief while we fought the other two.'

'And the other two?'

'Got away.'

'Bad luck. Looks like he needs the doc—'

'We called in on the doc on our way over,' Pitman said.

'Seems to me, you've both got everything covered.' Hopkins stood up. 'You know, Clint, for a blind man, you're mighty handy with a six-gun.'

'I wasn't always blind.' He hitched his holster.

'Yeah.' Hopkins noticed that it had been switched around; the gun was now on his right hip, the Dragoon butt facing across Clint's body. For a quick left-hand draw?

He unhooked the jailhouse keys and said to Dave, 'Empty your pockets!'

Dave obeyed, dropping on to the desk a pocketknife, a plug of tobacco, and a hundred dollars.

As he led him into the jailhouse, the sheriff said,

'Behave yourself, Dave. You're in a cell next to a lady.'

A few seconds later, Hopkins came out again. 'He says his pals from the Lazy-W will be back to break him out. Is that true?'

'Yes, that's what they said.'

Hopkins turned to the rifle rack, unlocked it. 'Pits, can you go and raise my deputy?'

'Sure.'

Pitman and Clint left the office and almost bumped into Dr Trask who was wearing his disgruntled face. He started at sight of Clint. 'I thought I told you to rest.'

'Don't worry, Doc. Your memory's not going. You told me, all right. But I can't sleep. I keep worrying about my wife.' Clint looked up the street at the big house, the upstairs lights glimmering.

Then he and Pitman descended the steps and turned to walk downtown to get the sheriff's deputy, Clay.

Drowsy and a little restless, Belle lay on top of the bed covers. Crouched at the bedside, Mrs Kilbride whispered in Belle's ear: 'I never truly loved my husband. . . .' Her voice was low, hoarse, disguised; she enjoyed this part very much. 'Clint was a liar and a cheat. I hate him. He gambled away our money and our home. . . .'

Irritatingly, Gamlin paced to and fro at the foot of the bed, biting his lip. 'Why does it always go wrong? Don't I deserve her love?'

'Of course you do.' Mrs Kilbride stood, her heart melting at his distress, and moved to Gamlin's side. 'But you're moving too fast. Why the urgency?'

Gamlin's tongue flicked over his lips, as if he wanted to reveal some hidden fact. She wondered what it was. He glanced away. 'This one's strong willed. I don't know how

123

long I can keep her here unless. . . .'

'You made the same mistake with the last one in Missouri. Rushed her before she was pliant. It takes time for affection and love to grow, Jeremy.' Many years, she felt like adding; not that he had ever recognized her feelings for him.

As Clint and Pitman limped alongside Deputy Clay, they noticed four horsemen gathering outside the sheriff's office. 'I think our expected trouble has arrived,' said Pitman.

Clay nodded and levered a cartridge into the rifle's chamber. 'You two had better make yourselves scarce. I'll take it from here.'

'But—' Pitman said.

'This is a law issue. No need for you to get shot. Besides, there's only four. Sheriff Hopkins and I should be able to deal with them.'

Pitman was about to protest again when Clint's hand landed heavily on his shoulder. 'The deputy's right, Pits. Let's get out of harm's way.' He thumbed over his shoulder, to the same side of the street as the sheriff's office.

'Yeah, OK,' said Pitman. 'Good luck, Clay.'

'Thanks,' came the dry-throated reply.

Pitman helped Clint hurry to the boardwalk. They mounted the steps and limped along to the first alley. 'We're about forty feet from the jailhouse block,' Pitman said.

Clint nodded. 'We'll go round the back. While I admire Deputy Clay's optimism and faith in the rule of law, I suspect they've got more than four men set to spring our man.'

'OK.'

At the second alley they came to, Pitman noticed a pair of black horses idling in the traces of a funeral hearse. He mentioned it to Clint.

'Maybe the undertaker got advance bookings?'

'Very droll,' Pitman said.

They covered a little more ground then Pitman came to an abrupt halt and gently eased Clint into shadow. 'You were right,' he whispered. 'Two on a wagon – a yoke of oxen – they've got rope from the jail bars to the wagon. . . .'

'I guess they mean business.'

'What'll we do?'

'Stop them, of course.'

'I was afraid you'd say that.'

'Let Dave go, Sheriff, and we won't bother you again!' shouted Chad Martin, riding his horse up and down past the hitching rail. 'It was all a misunderstanding.' He waved his wounded left arm. 'I got shot, but it's my own fault, I had too much liquor! We'll pay the fine and call it quits, eh?'

'No way! There won't be any fine. He's been charged with attempted murder. He goes to trial!' Sheriff Hopkins watched from an office window, his rifle gripped tightly. Beside him crouched Dr Trask. He shook his head. 'Looks like you might be busy tonight, Doc.'

'Or the undertaker. . . .'

'Yeah, probably.' He called out, 'Go back to the ranch and leave this to the law!'

'Sorry, Sheriff. Can't do that. Promised Dave.'

'Promises, eh? All you men out there, I'm giving you fair warning. Once the shooting starts, I can't *promise* I'll be taking any prisoners!'

One of the horsemen laughed.

'Do as the sheriff says!' ordered Deputy Clay. He stood to the left of the office, in the middle of the street.

'What's all that noise?' Mrs Kilbride demanded, rising from Belle's bedside.

Gamlin strode over to the window. Reflections from the lamp made it difficult to make out precisely what was happening. 'Probably a group of rowdies outside the sheriff's office. Nothing that need concern us.'

He gestured at Belle, her sleeping features contorted in some dreamlike distress. 'Let's get on with it.'

'I still think we should slow down.'

'I'd rather not,' he said. 'If only we could make her forget she was ever married – then she'd welcome me, my wealth and my love.' He paced over to Mrs Kilbride and gently grabbed her arm. 'I have so much love to give.'

'I know,' she said, her voice thick with emotion.

The thickset stern-faced cowboy, Ian Kinney, was as sore as a skinned coon. His wounded leg ached; probably he'd be crippled for life, like that no-hoper Pitman. Anger fuelled with whiskey impelled him to pull his Navy Colt. He shot Deputy Clay.

'Oh, no!' groaned Sheriff Hopkins and aimed and fired at Kinney.

Clay slumped to his knees, staring disbelievingly at blood oozing from his left arm.

Seconds later, Kinney sprawled beside him, lifeless eyes staring up.

Then all hell broke loose.

The rope tautened between the jailhouse bars and the

wagon, as the two men urged the oxen to pull. Sounds of gunfire and bullets ricocheting on the other side of the building echoed down the alleyway.

'They're twenty feet away, dead ahead,' Pitman whispered to Clint. 'Elevation 25 degrees.'

On their way here, Clint had said, 'If you can give me a bead on a target, I'd appreciate it.'

'Sure, Clint.'

'But none of that artillery jargon with quadrant elevation and azimuth. Keep it basic.'

'I'll try. . . . You know, Clint, you're full of surprises. Full of them.'

Now, Clint said, 'OK, I've got them covered.' He stood side-on, Dragoon in his left hand. 'Make your play.'

'Hey, guys, put a brake on that wagon. That's an order!' barked Pitman, his Buntline pointing at the backs of the two men. 'And turn real slow in case I get any ideas and shoot you between the shoulder blades.'

The man on the right slammed his foot on the brake and the wagon groaned. Then the pair of them raised their hands. 'Take it easy, we're only doing what boss Martin tells us.'

'Jump down off there!' Pitman ordered.

'No,' Clint whispered hoarsely, but too late.

As the men jumped either side of the wagon, they went for their guns and turned, firing.

Clint continued to stand left side on to them, presenting a narrower target.

Pitman fired at the man on the left, furthest away, and missed. The man on the right fired at Pitman; maybe it was a lucky shot – his slug hit Pitman's gun-hand and he dropped the weapon. 'For Pete's sake, run!' Pitman yelled at Clint.

Clint stood like a statue, biding his time. The flash from the gun on the right was faintly discernible and he returned fire accurately. The man stumbled back, clutching his belly. The gunman on their left fired at Pitman and Clint, splitting his concentration, which was his undoing. Pitman called, 'Ten o'clock, ten degrees el!' Clint swivelled on his heels, moving counter-clockwise, and fired.

The man lurched forward on his face.

'Nice shooting.'

'Pretty good sighting, thanks,' said Clint, helping Pitman to his feet. 'Let's get out front and help the sheriff.'

Pitman reached down and retrieved his Buntline, holstered it.

As they limped back the way they'd come, Clint said, 'How's the hand?'

'Bloody, sore, and I can't shoot a gun. I'm sorry.'

'But you can ride a rig?'

'Yeah, why?'

Clint stopped and Pitman stumbled into him. Clint gestured to his right. 'It's about here, isn't it?'

Pitman stared at the funeral hearse, the horses facing towards the Main Street alley opening. Then he glanced the way they'd come. 'How'd you. . . ? Never mind.'

In seconds, they'd clambered onboard the hearse. 'I don't reckon we can do any damage,' Clint said, releasing the brake, 'but we can create a distraction that'll give the sheriff a chance to pick them off.'

'Nothing new there, then. Artillerymen are used to being prime targets!' Pitman lashed the whip over the horses' heads.

The hearse rumbled into the main street, the horses snorting, black plumes waving, and bore down on the three Lazy-W men shooting from the cover of a water trough and an empty wagon, Clint firing at the sound of their guns.

Pitman gritted his teeth and prayed. One man moved out from cover and levelled his pistol to shoot, but a blast from the sheriff's rifle laid him low. Another tried hiding from Clint's blazing revolver and scuttled into the path of the sheriff's next bullet.

'All right, it's over!' shouted Chad Martin. He discarded his revolver and stood up.

Clint stopped firing and holstered his Dragoon.

Pitman eased the hearse to a halt facing Martin.

'A hearse?' queried Sheriff Hopkins as he stepped out on to the porch.

'Seemed appropriate, considering,' Clint said.

Both of them limped down Main Street. Clint carried the Buntline in his right hand and the Dragoon in his left.

'I bet we look a strange pair,' Pitman said.

'If anybody was out watching, perhaps we would.'

'Oh, someone's watching all right.' Pitman looked at the big house at the end of the street. Its lights gave a buttery glow through the many windows.

'Seems quite welcoming, doesn't it?'

'How much can you see, Clint?'

'Pinpricks of yellow, four above three.'

'Maybe we should wait for the sheriff.'

'He's got his hands full clearing up that mess behind us. I've waited long enough.' He stopped walking but never moved his eyes from those seven lights. 'You don't have to come with me. You've been a great help; I don't want your death on my conscience.'

'Who said anything about getting killed? We drive

129

hearses, we don't ride *in* them!'

'Just be careful. I don't know what this Gamlin fellow's capable of. . . .' He bit his lip. 'I only pray we're in time.'

Gamlin and Mrs Kilbride stood at the window, transfixed by the gunfight outside the sheriff's office. 'I wonder what that's about,' mused Mrs Kilbride, her long thin hands fidgeting.

'Drunks shooting up the place, I imagine.'

Mrs Kilbride glanced towards Belle. She was right, he thought as he took one last glance out the window, we should get on with—

Then his eyes started and a hand of steel grasped his heart and squeezed.

He gasped as if winded by a massive punch and stepped back from the window. 'Oh, my God, it's him – he's coming!'

'Who?'

'Her dead husband, that's who!'

'You mean he isn't dead? You went to all that trouble, and he's still alive?'

'Yes, dammit, woman, yes!'

'You knew he was here, didn't you? That's why you've been so anxious to hurry!'

'Yes, but he should have been shot in his sleep by now . . . I paid—'

'Oh, Jeremy.'

'What can I do?' he wailed.

'Dowse the lights,' she said, 'he might go away.'

'Yes, that's it. If we don't answer, we're not in!'

They rushed round, putting out the lamps, plunging the other upstairs rooms into darkness.

Hands shaking with the onset of fear, Gamlin retrieved his rifle from under the stairs. Somehow, he managed to lever a shell into the breach. He mounted the first tread of the staircase.

'I thought you couldn't face killing a man?' Mrs Kilbride said, a hand on the newel post. 'That's why you employed that gang to murder Belle's husband.'

He turned. 'That's true. But if they don't go away, I need more time and this will buy it for me. I've just got to stay strong. Will you help me?' He hated pleading, especially to her.

After a few seconds' hesitation, she nodded. 'Very well. But you must promise that if this woman doesn't fulfil your dreams, then you will stop.'

He looked away. There was only a single lamp on in the lobby. The sides were shrouded in deep shadows. The darkness was his friend, he knew. He felt safe in the dark. Maybe because his wife Lydia had embraced the darkness when she left this mortal coil. In the dark, he felt close to her in spirit. Yes, but he wanted to be close to her in the flesh too. Could he give up, if this one – what was her name? – if Belle failed to replace Lydia? No, he couldn't stop. Never! 'Yes, I promise, this one is the last,' he lied.

They climbed the stairs together. A single oil lamp glowed on the landing. They entered Belle's bedroom.

While Mrs Kilbride turned off the bedside lamp, he opened the sash window wider and slowly slid the barrel out over the sill.

CHAPTER THIRTEEN

WALLED UP

Pitman's keen eyes spotted the movement and identified the barrel as it emerged. 'Two o'clock, elevation 45 degrees!'

Clint estimated, raised his Dragoon, pointed the seven-and-a-half inch barrel, and fired.

His shot shattered the window and the rifle barrel jerked up and fired then was pulled back inside, into the dark.

'Good shooting!'

'Move her,' Mrs Kilbride said, her voice deep and ghostly in the dark. 'If she isn't here, he can't do a thing. . . .'

'But why's he coming here, how'd he know?'

'Forget that for now! You've got to carry her, take her to the basement!'

'What, you've. . .?'

'Yes, I prepared the place, just in case it didn't work out.'

'You didn't want it to work out, did you?'

132

'Now, Jeremy, don't be like that.'

'I haven't got time for this now.' Still clutching the rifle, he picked up the unconscious Belle, and strode towards the door. 'Open the damned door, woman!'

They hurried out on to the landing. Mrs Kilbride switched off the oil lamp. As they descended the stairs, the landing creaked and moaned in darkness. The lobby lamp was extinguished, then the kitchen.

The basement door was under the stairs. Mrs Kilbride opened it and lantern light shone up the stone steps. Gamlin squeezed past her and hurried down, breathing heavily with the weight of Belle in his arms. At the bottom, he hesitated a few seconds, eyeing a newly erected false wall, the cement still gleaming wetly in the lamplight. Then he laid Belle on a mattress behind this wall. On a cupboard at the bedhead was a carafe of water and a glass.

'If necessary, we can brick her up later,' Mrs Kilbride said.

He glared at her. 'You think of everything, don't you?'

'My pleasure,' she said and received a sour look.

Faintly, he heard the doorknocker.

'Why are you knocking when he's as good as taken a pot-shot at you?' Pitman asked.

'Good point,' Clint said and slammed his foot against the door.

The faint glow at the bottom of the door went out. 'They've just put out the last light,' Pitman said.

'That's a bad move. Now they're as blind as I am.'

At the first sound of the knocker, Gamlin gripped his rifle and climbed up the basement steps. When he reached the top, he turned. 'When she regains consciousness, give her some water and take care of her till I get back.'

'Yes, of course,' Mrs Kilbride said.

He shut the door on her and no light leaked out. He ran back into the dark passage leading to the kitchen door, bouncing off the walls in the darkness. Once in the kitchen, he bumped into the table and worked his way round it until he found the knob and swung open the back door.

Welcome moonlight beamed in through the doorway, affording him some illumination. He sat at the huge wood table. From here, he had an uninterrupted view of the front door and lobby. He jacked another cartridge into the chamber.

The door parted from its hinges at Clint's second kick and fell noisily into the lobby. As the echoing sound died, the house grew silent.

Clint hugged the left side of the doorjamb. Pitman was outside against the wall.

'I can't hear any movement,' Clint whispered and hurried inside, over the fallen door that wobbled on its internal handle.

A rifle blazed up ahead somewhere, the muzzle flash too distant, too fast for his poor left eye to register its exact position. As the doorjamb to his left splintered and sprayed his shoulder with wood, Clint dived to the left and rolled on the tiled floor, his wounded thigh screaming in protest over this precipitate exertion. Then he stopped moving and listened.

He heard his own breathing, and attempted to calm it.

Could do with Mutt right now – instead, the dog was tethered to the bedpost in the hotel room.

'I don't know who you are,' Gamlin shouted, 'but

you're intruding on my property! The law'll be here any minute!'

'You must be Jeremy Gamlin,' Clint said. 'And I think you know who I am.'

'You'll be under arrest any minute, I warn you!'

'The law's on my side, Gamlin. I'm here to collect my wife!'

The unholy racket up in the lobby sent Mrs Kilbride's heart hammering. She glared at the comatose form of Belle Brennan and blamed her for their current misfortune. She should never have come to this house, a home she'd lovingly prepared for Jeremy. She didn't fit in here! As long as she lived, he'd be besotted with her, and try to mould her into a copy of Lydia.

Her fingers opened and clenched and she realized she was clasping a pillow. This was the answer, the only option. She walked to the bedside and leaned over Belle.

Most of the quacks out west wouldn't know a suffocation case anyway, so Belle's death could easily be passed off as natural.

Mrs Kilbride lowered the pillow over Belle's face.

A fusillade of shots peppered the fallen door in the lobby but no ricochet or splinter hit Clint.

'Pits, I need to see him!' Clint called from the left of the passage that led to the kitchen door. 'Can you do that for me?'

'Yes, I have an idea. Two minutes!'

Clint fired once into the passage, just to dissuade Gamlin from venturing forward. Gamlin has no idea I'm blind, he thought, so he won't take any chances.

It was a long two minutes; he wondered how long it

seemed to Gamlin.

Suddenly, a loud crash of shattered glass came from the kitchen, followed by the unmistakeable smell of kerosene and the crackling of flames. Pits had torched the kitchen!

Clint limped out from concealment, his left side to the passage. His heart leapt as his solitary eye identified the light from the flames, set in a rectangle of black. And now, in the middle of the light, a blurred black silhouette. Clint fired, just once; the sound of his Dragoon briefly bounced off the passage walls. The silhouette crumpled and fell away from Clint's vision.

Was Gamlin hit, was he dead, or was he playing possum?

'Jeremy!' For an instant, Mrs Kilbride eased off the pillow, as if her heaving heart knew instinctively that he'd been shot.

Gasping for air, Belle slammed her fists at the side of Mrs Kilbride's head. The sudden surprise attack unsettled the older woman and she tumbled sideways off the bed. Coughing on precious air, Belle rolled on to the floor and stood, massaging her neck. 'You tried to kill me!'

Rising from the floor, Mrs Kilbride snarled, 'I'll more than try, you strumpet!' She strode round the bed, her eyes darting, fierce. She clutched the pillow in front of her.

Belle snatched the carafe of water and flung its contents at Mrs Kilbride's face. As the woman faltered and spluttered, Belle pressed home her attack, shoving the pillow down with her left hand and sweeping her right hand round. The carafe shattered against Mrs Kilbride's head and the woman staggered back. But as she stumbled, a claw-like hand grabbed Belle's wrist.

The pair of them staggered and thudded into the false wall.

Mrs Kilbride's fingers reached out, clawing at Belle's eyes.

Belle pulled her head away while at the same time thrusting the housekeeper against the wall.

It started to give; cracks in the grouting snaked up and across.

Bricks dislodged from the top and bashed Belle's arm. She let go of Mrs Kilbride and shoved herself away.

Abruptly, in the blinking of her eye, the wall tumbled down on top of Mrs Kilbride.

The place was clogged with brick and cement dust and the cloying smell of damp earth and plaster. Pushing the wounded Gamlin ahead, Clint called, 'Belle, are you there?'

'Clint? But I saw you—'

'I've got her – it's all right, ma'am, it's me, Charles Edward Pitman, late of the artillery. . . .'

'That's enough introductions, Pits. Watch our prisoner while I hug my wife!'

Covered in dust, they crossed the rubble-strewn floor and embraced.

'Oh, Clint, it's so good to hold you again!' She pushed herself back, and he guessed she was staring at his face. 'Your eyes!'

He pulled her tight to him, kissed her forehead. 'I'm kinda blind right now, but I'll be all right, it'll pass,' he said, trying to inject confidence into his voice. 'I found you, didn't I?'

Her hands ran delicately over his features. 'Tell me, Clint. Tell me everything.'

'Later. Seems to me, we've now got all the time in the world.'

The dust had settled when Doc Trask climbed down, accompanied by Sheriff Hopkins.

Gamlin knelt beside Mrs Kilbride. He and Pitman had scrabbled to remove the bricks from her body.

'Oh, my God, I can smell burning!' Belle exclaimed.

'It's the kitchen,' said the sheriff, 'but the townspeople have it under control.'

Doc Trask put a hand on Gamlin's shoulder. 'Sorry, sir, but she's too badly damaged internally.'

'I heard that, Doctor.' Mrs Kilbride grimaced and stared at Gamlin.

Gamlin let out a sob. 'You can't leave me, we've still got work to do, we've got to find another Lydia.'

Her dust- and blood-covered hand raised to his face, stroked his cheek, where fresh stubble had formed.

'Foolish boy, I think you've tried too many times already,' she whispered hoarsely, tear-streaks snaking into the dust on her cheeks. 'You know, I loved you the first day I came to your family home as governess and nurse. . . .'

Gamlin stared. 'Loved me? But you're – you're at least ten years older. . . .'

She let out a hoarse laugh. 'Age has no dominion over love, my boy.' She coughed up blood. 'I'm sorry, I couldn't let Lydia have you. . . .'

'I don't understand. What do you mean?'

'How'd your wife Lydia die?' Belle asked.

'The doctor said she had a fainting fit while out riding. A horrible accident.'

'I made it look like an accident,' Mrs Kilbride said.

'You – you?'

'If only I'd known then how obsessed you'd become, I mightn't have done it . . . What irony, eh?' She stared up at Clint and a frown creased her forehead. 'Are you the one –

Belle's husband?'

'Yes,' he said curtly.

'But you're blind. . . .'

'So?'

'Yet you beat us.'

Belle hugged him, her voice thick with sobs. 'His love kept him going.'

'You're both very lucky to have found love. So many never encounter it,' Mrs Kilbride said. Then life abandoned her grimy features.

CHAPTER FOURTEEN

LIFE'S CHEAP

Sheriff Hopkins, flanked by Pitman and Clint, entered the Wedlock bank and approached Mr Walsh's desk.

'Good morning, Sheriff,' said Walsh, standing up. 'Quite a night you had, by all accounts.' He offered his hand.

The sheriff ignored the gesture and withdrew from his jacket a couple of paper bank receipts. 'I got these papers while investigating a crime, Mr Walsh.'

'Really, Sheriff? They look like our bank receipts.'

'They are. I'm here to examine your dealings with Mr Gamlin.'

Walsh smiled but shook his head. 'Sorry, but our customers warrant complete privacy. It's our bank's motto: Integrity before God.'

Clint drew his Dragoon and held it inches away from Walsh's face. 'In which case, let's call this a bank robbery. I'm here to steal information about Gamlin.'

Chin wobbling, Walsh eyed the sheriff. 'You can't let him do this!'

'I don't see a thing,' the sheriff said.

'You're not afraid of a blind man, are you, Mr Walsh?' Pitman said.

For a second, Walsh stared at Clint then his face lost its colour. 'Oh, my God, he is, isn't he? He won't know where he's shooting. . . .'

'Just keep talking, and I'll have a pretty good idea,' Clint said.

Walsh clamped his mouth shut. His eyes widened, showing whites all round them.

'I'll make it easier for you, Mr Walsh,' said the sheriff. 'We've got Gamlin locked up on several charges. He's unlikely to see much of the rest of his life outside prison. Now, about that information?'

'Oh, really?' Shakily, Walsh extracted a handkerchief and dabbed at his forehead. 'You know, I thought there was something shifty about him all along. I'm a fair judge of character, you know.'

'But you dealt with him, nonetheless?' Clint said.

'He was giving me money. . . .'

'That's what we want to talk to you about,' said the sheriff.

Walsh nodded at the papers. 'You've got the receipts, it's all legal.'

'Maybe, but I have reason to believe the money he paid you and deposited was stolen from the Bethesda Falls bank.'

'Oh, my God.' Walsh sank on to his seat and swallowed.

'And to preserve your bank's motto, I think you'd better hand it over as evidence. I'll give you a receipt, of course.'

141

'All of it? The purchase money for the house as well?'

'Yes, all of it.'

Somehow, Walsh's face managed to turn even paler.

A while later, they gathered outside the sheriff's office. Clint sat astride Taffy, his left hand gripping the leash of Mutt. The bags of money were secured to his saddle horn and in the saddle-bags. Mounted on Yankee, Belle rode beside him. Pitman drove the buckboard with the hand-cuffed and chained Molly and Gamlin secured to the flatbed. Bringing up the rear was Deputy Clay, his left arm amply bandaged. Beatrice the donkey was tethered to the rear of the buckboard.

Sheriff Hopkins stood on the boardwalk, arms akimbo. 'Doc Trask and I searched their rooms and came up with a few interesting items.'

'You had no right!' snapped Gamlin.

'I'm the law, Mr Gamlin. I have every right.'

'What did you find?' Clint asked.

'Bottles of drugs. From what you've said, Mrs Brennan, it seems like they were doping you up.'

She nodded. 'That explains the dizziness.'

'Yes, Doc Trask confirms it, that's one side-effect. . . .'

She shook her head. 'For a few moments, I was convinced I was losing my mind. At other times, I really believed Clint had ruined us. . . .'

'Anything else?' Clint asked.

'Six envelopes, with names on them.'

'They're mine!' Gamlin protested.

'Were. Now, they're evidence,' said the sheriff. 'If I recollect, their names were Lydia, Marianne, Alice, Chantel, Harriet and Belle; each contained a lock of hair – similar to yours in colour, Mrs Brennan.'

'My God, he – he failed with them – and disposed of them, didn't he?'

'Looks that way, ma'am. Soon as he's given evidence in Bethesda about the bank job, we'll be wanting him back here. I reckon I'll have a few telegraph messages to send.' He pulled out a slip of paper from his jeans. 'Which reminds, me, I've telegraphed Bethesda Falls. Confidential, of course, so nobody else has any idea you're carrying a lot of money. Right now, I reckon they've got one very happy bank manager!'

Hayes was far from pleased to hear that both Molly and Gamlin were being brought back alive. He met Trent and Howie on horseback in the alley next to the bank and explained.

'So, Rutherford, they're returning for trial – with the money. And if Molly and Gamlin talk, you know where that leaves you two, eh?'

'Yeah, I guess we do. What did you have in mind?'

Hayes gave them an avuncular smile. 'If they were to have an accident, it might prove financially rewarding for you both.'

'I understand,' said Howie. He ground his teeth together. 'It'll be a pleasure, Mr Hayes.'

Riding out of town stirrup-to-stirrup, Trent said, 'What'd he mean, "financially rewarding"? Does that mean we get to keep the money?'

'He might not have meant that, but that's my understanding, Trent.' He scowled. 'She shouldn't have run out on us like that, you know. We made a good team, the two of us.'

'But we make a good team, too, don't we, Howie?'

143

Howie slapped a hand on Trent's back. 'Better!'

'It's your fault, you must have told him about me!' snapped Gamlin, rattling his chains in the back of the buckboard.

'I told him I robbed the bank, that's all,' Molly said. 'He asked me why we took his wife, but I didn't answer. I didn't know – still don't.' She glared at him. 'What was all that about, back there? Those women's names?'

Gamlin shook his head. 'Nothing, nothing.' How did it all go wrong? He thought back to a week or so ago, when he'd been paired up with Molly Nelson at the Bella Union. The night had been one of the best he'd experienced. He soon gathered that she was a tough nut and when she let drop that she and her friends were always looking for well-paid work, he asked, 'What kind of work?'

'We do anything, Mr Gamlin. We're not particular. Anything at all.'

'Would your gang kill for me, if I paid well?'

'Sure. You may have noticed, life's cheap round here.' She grinned. 'But me and the boys ain't cheap. If you want a good job done, it'll cost you.'

He sat up, oblivious of her state of undress, his eyes darting to a table. He got out of the bed, snatched a notebook from his jacket and sat down at the table. 'I want you to kill a homesteader called Clint Brennan. Here's where his place is.' He swiftly sketched a map of the town and the position of the Brennan home.

'Easy.'

'I also want you to abduct his wife, Belle.'

'Ah, now that might not be so easy. If she's kept alive, she can identify us to the law. We could end up with our necks stretched.'

144

He swung round in his chair. 'I've just thought of an inducement you can't refuse. Brilliant, really!'

'Go on, I'm all ears.'

He grinned. 'All of a lot of things, from where I'm sitting.'

'Stick to the business, Mr Gamlin.'

'Very well. For your payment, I'll help you rob the bank I work at.'

Her eyes widened. She got up and sat opposite him at the table. 'This gets more interesting by the second.'

'I'll give you the times and everything. You or your men empty the safe, pretend to go north, then head south to the Brennan place. Kill the husband and abduct the woman.' He jabbed his pencil on a cross on his rough map. 'I'll meet with you here, at an old shack, on the second night.'

She leaned across and shook his hand. 'You've got a deal!'

'But your men must think it's your idea, not mine. I have to appear an innocent party in all this.'

'No problem.' She hesitated, her head to one side. 'What's to stop us killing you and running off with the money – without killing Brennan or taking his wife?'

'I'll have taken money from the safe the night before your robbery. That's your bonus – providing you don't kill anyone during the robbery and you deliver the woman to me *untouched*.'

'You've thought of everything, I guess. When do we fill in the details?'

'Tomorrow night. Repeat performance?'

'Oh, you saucy thing. You businessmen are all alike!'

Of course, he'd barely left a third of the contents of the safe for them to rob; the rest, he cached. When he approached their hideout, he fired his rifle at the shack – that at least was a target he could hit – and pretended to be the posse. Molly knocked Belle unconscious then came out with her two men, assuring them that it was all right. She wasn't that trusting, however, as her Smith & Wesson was cocked and ready.

'Is she in there?' he'd asked.

Molly nodded. 'Out cold. Now, where's our bonus?'

Keeping the rifle trained on them, he gestured with the barrel at a sack hanging on a tree some five feet to the right. 'As agreed. Now you ride.'

'Suits us,' said Molly, retrieving the money sack. The two men peered inside and whistled.

Then the three of them mounted their horses and rode out, tailing the two Brennan mounts.

When he reckoned they were well away, he rushed over to the shack and opened the door. Belle lay unconscious in her underwear, with her hands tied, but otherwise she seemed unharmed. He stared at her form, her beauty. Now, lying there, she had the same effect on him he'd experienced when she walked into the bank that day with her husband. The resemblance to Lydia was uncanny. That weekend, he'd ridden out to Wedlock to talk with Mrs Kilbride and she'd said, 'You know I find it difficult to deny you anything, Master Gamlin. But this must be your last attempt. . . .'

The horses whinnied and the dog growled and Gamlin started out of his reverie, realizing what she'd done, what he'd done, all in the name of love.

'Something's wrong up ahead,' Clint said.

Deputy Clay said, 'I'll go and investigate.'

'What is it?' Belle asked as the deputy rode off.

'I can smell smoke,' said Clint.

146

'Smoke?' queried Pitman.

'Yes.' He turned in the saddle, its leather creaking. 'Mutt, up on the wagon!'

Pitman shuffled along on the bench seat for Mutt and scrutinized the slight rise ahead. The blue sky seemed to transform as the first wisps of grey-brown drifted across. 'Prairie fire!' he shouted.

'Wait, steady!' Clint warned. 'Let's see where the flames are coming from.' He lifted his head, sniffed the air. 'The wind's northwest, so we should turn in that direction.'

Slowly, Pitman edged the wagon's horses over to his right.

'Belle, stay with me.' He passed her a loop from his lariat. 'Whatever happens, I'm not losing you again.'

'I'll be with you, Clint, have no fear.'

'OK. Let's ride!' Clint bawled.

Pitman snaked the whip over the horses' heads and they rode at full gallop, veering to the northwest. Within a few minutes, Pitman saw the deputy returning through swirling grey, the lower half of his face concealed by a bandana, his horse's eyes wide and wild.

Deputy Clay lowered his cloth mask. 'A broad stretch of grass and trees ahead is on fire. The smoke's building.' He pointed. 'You're heading in the right direction, should miss most of it – unless the wind changes.'

'Did you see anybody?' Clint demanded.

'Eh, what're you driving at?' Pitman said.

'I've got a suspicious nature, is all,' Clint said. 'I just reckon that a fire starting up about now on our route seems to be a mighty big coincidence.'

'No, not a soul,' Clay replied.

'Right,' Clint said, 'let's stop for a minute or two and

147

cover the eyes of our horses. They won't care much for the smoke, but flames will panic them. And cover mouths and noses best you can.'

'Is that the best you could come up with?' demanded Howie.

Trent's eyes glinted, his grin broad. 'Yeah, it's a beauty, ain't it?'

'If that damned fire burns our targets, it'll also burn the money!'

Trent swore. 'I never thought about that.'

'Yeah, well, it's done now. If we can jump them as they come through the smoke, we can still get the money.'

'If we can see them.'

'Yeah. And whose fault is that?'

Trent's grin froze.

The wind had veered and the smoke suddenly engulfed the pair.

Everyone was riding blind, coughing into their bandanas. The smoke was cloying and had a damping effect on sounds too. Clint could hardly hear the wagon wheels nearby. For a second, he feared that Pitman had hit a rock and overturned – easily done in this situation.

But he couldn't stop. And he was reassured by the constant tug of Belle on the lariat. So far, according to Belle, they hadn't encountered any naked flames yet. Taffy strained over the uneven ground, his hoofs thundering on the burnt grass that sent up a strange crisp crinkling sound.

Without warning, he heard a voice, getting closer. Whooping, as if the man was on a cattle drive.

Disembodied.

Ahead.

None of his party was ahead so... Clint drew his Dragoon and fired at the approaching hollering sound.

The gun's report was muffled.

A high-pitched scream followed, then they were riding on, nothing else to distract him.

CHAPTER FIFTEEN

FINAL RECKONING

Out of the smoke loomed a figure on horseback, pistol drawn. Pitman heaved on the reins to veer the horses to the right. The mysterious rider edged his mount closer, closer still, the lower part of his face concealed with a bandana. His sombrero brim was bent back with the force of the wind.

To control the horses needed every ounce of energy Pitman possessed; he couldn't stop or risk reaching for his gun; his hand was still useless anyway. Mutt sat on the seat, hackles up, growling, but the distance from wagon to rider was too great for him to jump.

'Molly, you bitch,' bawled the intruder, 'we had it all!'

'Howie!' shrieked Molly.

'Why'd you run off?'

'Don't do this. I was abducted!'

Howie laughed. 'I've heard that one before!' Smoke swirled and thickened as he fired into the back of the buckboard. In the same instant, the vehicle lurched and Mutt leapt to the ground.

Must have hit a boulder, Pitman thought as, seconds later, the buckboard tipped on its side. Wood and metal groaned and parted company. Cries of pain and despair swamped his ears.

Pitman was pulled clear by the reins. As he hit the ground, he grazed his knees and elbows then let go. He rolled over, not a second too soon, as one of the displaced wagon wheels pounded out of the smoke towards him. He dodged behind the offending boulder in time. The wheel hit the stone and jumped into the air.

He pulled out his Buntline with his left hand. Coughing and wheezing for air, he limped towards the wrecked vehicle.

Molly had been thrown several feet away. He checked her throat: she was unconscious but otherwise seemed unhurt. Howie's shot must have missed her; not surprising in the swirling smoke. He dashed to the splintered buckboard. Gamlin sat with his back against the upturned wooden bed, holding his head and groaning. A fresh bullet wound showed on his shoulder; so Howie's slug went wild a bit, missed Molly and hit Gamlin, who now had two shoulder injuries.

Then Pitman located Howie, trapped under his dead horse, a huge piece of wood from the wagon sticking out of the animal's chest. Mutt gripped Howie's gun hand and savagely tugged. 'Get him off of me!' Howie wailed then coughed on the smoke. He swore. 'That stupid Trent and his damned fires!'

Gradually, the smoke dissipated as the fire burned itself out. Between them, Pitman, Clay and Belle secured Howie on one buckboard horse, and Molly and Gamlin on the other. Clay had ridden back about half a mile and located the body of Trent: Clint's shot had been surprisingly accurate, hitting the man's lung: he'd probably died from smoke inhalation, however. Now, with Pitman's help, Clay lifted the body on to Howie's horse. His face pale, Howie turned away.

At that moment, Deputy Sheriff Johnson rode up. 'Howdy. I came out to investigate the smoke – in case I needed to alert the town fire brigade.'

'The fire blew itself out,' Deputy Clay said.

Pointing at the wrecked buggy, Johnson said, 'Seems you've had a bit of bad luck.'

'Nothing to do with luck,' Deputy Clay said. 'We were ambushed.'

'Really?'

'Yes.'

'Say, aren't you the deputy of Wedlock?'

'Yes. I thought you'd be expecting us.'

Johnson shook his head. 'Nope. Why would I?'

Clay pursed his lips and exchanged a look at Belle and Pitman. 'Sheriff Hopkins telegraphed Mr Hayes, the bank manager. Told him we were bringing in two of the bank robbers, plus the stolen money.'

Johnson whistled then grinned.

'While that information is confidential,' said Clint, 'I'd have thought Hayes would tell you to expect some prisoners.'

'Aren't you Clint Brennan?' Johnson said. Clint nodded then Johnson noticed Belle and tipped his hat. 'Mrs Brennan.'

'We can explain once we've got these three locked up,' Clint said.

'Three? But that's Mr Gamlin, from the bank!'

'As I said, we'll explain. For now, let's get going. We're due a final reckoning.'

152

Molly, Howie and Gamlin were locked up. Doc Will Strang treated Gamlin's new wound. Pitman, Belle, deputies Clay and Johnson sat round the sheriff's desk, sipping coffee laced with brandy. Hayes sat at the sheriff's desk, smoking a cigar. The saddle-bags crammed with the stolen money made a large pile on the desk.

Johnson said, 'You don't look too pleased to get your money back, Mr Hayes.'

Hayes shrugged and blew out smoke. 'Oh, I assure you, I am. It's the terrible things that happened as a consequence of the robbery, not least the loss of life.' He shook his head. 'I still can't understand how Gamlin was involved.'

'I don't know what happened to Gamlin,' Clint said, 'but on his way here he was quite forthcoming on a few points of interest.'

'Points of interest?' Hayes said.

'What did he say?' Johnson asked.

'Quite a bit. Some twenty years ago, the government passed the Townsite Act. It meant that a group of town-makers could get 320 acres at $1.25 an acre.'

'Sure,' Johnson said, 'we all know that. I imagine that's how Bethesda Falls started.'

'Well, Belle recalled reading in a newspaper that the government's now of the opinion that the deal's too generous to speculators. Next year they're going to pass a revised act.'

'So?'

'Only groups of at least 100 persons can qualify to claim. You're unlikely to find that many speculators in any one area or town.'

'I don't see how that affects us here,' Hayes said.

Clint said, 'According to Gamlin—'

'But you've just said,' Hayes interrupted, 'he's a liar and a crook. How can we trust anything he says?'

'I thought you'd say something like that, Mr Hayes, considering you've been siphoning off money from the town's funds to speculate on a new township – somewhere out past Rapid Creek – to be called Hayes City.'

Hayes shook his head. 'But the new rule, I couldn't—'

'Yes you could. You and the mayor simply invent names for prospective settlers.'

'My God, the mayor as well?' Johnson exclaimed.

'That's why I'm bringing it up here,' Clint said. 'I don't know how many other important townsmen are involved. Once you start this, there's no telling where it will end. Are you prepared for that?'

'Sure I am!' Johnson stood and glared at Hayes. 'Why, that's town money, invested in the future of *this* town – not any new one with your name on it!'

'This is preposterous,' Hayes said, stubbing out his cigar. 'I won't listen to any more of this nonsense. You have no proof. Your accusations are founded on the word of a – a villain!' He stood up.

'Don't make a move for that door, Mr Hayes!' Johnson barked, drawing his revolver.

Hayes gesticulated. 'You can't listen to a – a blind man and a villain, Deputy Sheriff.'

'You wanted proof?' Clint said. 'Well, we were ambushed by two men – who happened to be the original robbers of your bank.'

'They were?' squeaked Hayes.

'Yes. You paid them to ambush us.' Clint held up a hand. 'You can't wriggle out of this. You were the only recipient of the telegraph message telling you that we were coming here with two prisoners and the money.'

'But, that could be coincidence. . . .'

Clint shook his head. 'No, because Howie told us about your deal. And we have Doc Strang as a witness.'

'Doc Strang's one of the speculators. He wouldn't be so stupid. . . .'

'Yes, I was,' said Strang. 'But I didn't know where you got your money from, or that you were falsifying documentation to get round the new laws.'

Johnson grabbed the banker's upper arm. 'Come on, Mr Hayes – you've got company waiting back in the jail-house. I think you know them.'

As the deputy and his prisoner walked out of the office, Belle said, 'What about the mayor and the others?'

Clint shook his head. 'Don't rightly know. Maybe the town will start by electing a new mayor.'

'You may fit the bill,' suggested Pitman.

Clint let out a harsh laugh. 'I can't see worth a damn.'

'Well,' Pitman said, 'don't they say justice is blind?'

EPILOGUE

MONOCLE

As the days progressed, Clint found that his left eye wasn't blind. Indeed, with the help of Doc Strang's eye-drops, it gradually recovered some sight. He seemed to see everything as if down a tunnel, viewing the world through a tube. He and Belle stayed in town at the Constitution Hotel, courtesy of the town council, while friends went out to the farm to tidy and clean their home.

'I'm just popping out to see Oren,' he told Belle as she sat by the window with Susanna Moodie's *Life in the Clearings*. From here she had an uninterrupted view of the main street. Mutt lay at her feet, asleep.

'Is the eye-glass ready?'

He fitted a black patch over his blind right eye. 'Should be.'

'I'll watch out for you coming back, wearing it. My very own gentleman pirate.'

He leaned over her and kissed her lips. 'That tasted good,' he whispered.

'Yes, it did. Don't take too long, will you?'

'I won't, you can count on it,' he said and let himself out.

Carefully, Clint descended the staircase. The knack was not to look at his feet and the treads, since he'd become disoriented. When he'd had full sight, he never looked at his feet as he walked – he surveyed ahead for obstacles but let his feet do the walking. He must try to do that now.

He made it to Oren's and the two monocles were ready, each attached to a fine chain.

Clint fished in his vest pocket. 'How much do I owe you?'

'Nothing, it's my pleasure. You've saved our town's finances, it's the least I can do.'

'Well, thanks.'

'You know which is which?'

'Sure, I can feel the etching on this one.' Clint put it in the left-hand vest pocket. 'The other's plain.' That went into the other pocket.

'That's it,' Oren said.

'Coming down to the El Dorado?'

'No, thanks. Take care, now. There's usually a rough crowd, this part of the week.'

The El Dorado was less salubrious than The Gem but Clint preferred the earthy honesty of the place. No pretence. He entered and limped towards the bar counter. He was a regular and could have found it blindfold, or so Belle had said many a time. Even if he only allowed himself a single shot of whiskey a day. He was looking forward to one now.

Limping over the duckboards behind the counter, the bartender wore a salt-and-pepper moustache, a fairly white shirt and a lugubrious expression, though Clint couldn't see that too well; he was served from memory, however. 'What'll it be, stranger?' asked Billy the barkeep.

'Shot of bourbon – the usual,' Clint said.

Billy stared. 'Clint,' he whispered, 'is that you?'

'Yes.'

'What happened?' He gestured at Clint's left leg and his eye-patch.

'Long story. Where's my drink?'

'Sorry, coming right up.'

The tumbler was placed in front of him, and it smelled inviting, but Clint ignored it, drawn by the sound of a voice: 'Come on, gents, I'm not that sore a loser. Let me play a couple more hands, maybe I can win my money back, eh? What's fairer than that, eh?'

The speaker sat in a circle of card-players at the far end of the room.

Clint smiled, recognizing the voice. His single eye scanned the watching cowpokes standing round the table. The man on the extreme left with carrot hair seemed a likely candidate, he reckoned. All the rest Clint either knew or knew their type; trail-weary drifters. But the young man was different, held himself tense. Clint left his drink and walked into the centre of the floor area, and stood with his left side facing the group.

Slowly, deliberately, he took out the left-hand monocle and placed it in his left eye-socket. Etched on the glass were crosshairs, sight calibrations. At that moment, he decided that whenever he put this monocle on, he would have a target in mind.

'Gents,' he said, raising his voice above the general hubbub of the place, 'I recommend you stop playing cards with that man.'

A couple of chairs scraped back.

'Who the hell are you?' a card-player demanded.

'Actually, I'm the man who's calling Kevin Cafferty a cheat.'

As Cafferty rose to his feet, the card-players scrambled left and right, as far away as possible.

'I don't take kindly to that talk, Mister. I'll give you to the count of three to withdraw your ill-chosen remarks. One. . . .'

A hammer was cocked on Clint's left. His ears pricked and he heard Pitman whisper: 'Don't think about it, Mister. You don't want that hair to get any redder. This isn't your fight.'

'Two,' Clint said, knowing the red-haired man – doubtless Bart Begley – was now neutralized.

Cafferty hesitated, thrown off his own count. Then he blurted, 'Three!' He reached for his Buntline Navy revolver.

In one smooth swift motion, Clint's left hand crossed his body and drew his Dragoon from its holster and fired.

Cafferty jerked to one side and flung his weapon away, his shoulder bloody where the .44 slug penetrated. He stood, a hand clasped over his wound, and stared as Clint holstered his gun and limped towards him.

'Do I know you?'

'Oh, yes.' Clint grabbed Cafferty's wrist and the man hissed in pain. He tore off the cardsharp's shirtsleeve. A half-dozen playing cards tumbled to the floor. Watchers growled disapproval and someone whispered 'necktie.'

'There'll be no lynching in my town,' Deputy Johnson said at the door.

Cafferty swore. 'You're – you're the blind man?'

Clint nodded and turned to the assembled cowpokes.

'Let this be a lesson to you all,' he said. 'This man let you win a little, but in the end he intended robbing you blind.'